BROGAN: COWBOY PRIDE

THE KAVANAGH BROTHERS BOOK THREE

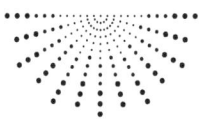

KATHLEEN BALL

Copyright © 2020 by Kathleen Ball

All rights reserved.

No part of this book may be reproduced in any form or by any electronic or mechanical means, including information storage and retrieval systems, without written permission from the author, except for the use of brief quotations in a book review.

❀ Created with Vellum

I dedicate Brogan: Cowboy Risk to my incredible, sweet, strong editor Kay Springsteen. Her indomitable spirit is an example to us all.

As always I dedicate this book to Bruce, Steven, Colt, Clara and Mavis because I love them.

CHAPTER ONE

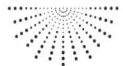

Brogan hurled his black hat onto the lush grass pasture. His horses were missing, not all but enough. The income from those horses was crucial to survive the winter. He stared at his dun, Prince. "Mind telling me where your friends went?"

The horse stared back and one of his ears twitched.

Grumbling, Brogan stalked across the grass and snatched up his hat. After a last look around, he jammed it on his head. Without those horses he wouldn't be able to feed the horses he planned to keep. A catastrophe this was, a foul catastrophe. He mounted up and turned Prince toward the far corner of the property.

He had to find those horses at all costs. Even if it meant his life. He'd rather starve than go back home with his hat in hand. Never would he step foot on the Kavanagh land again. His gut clenched. He had tried and struggled to push all thoughts of his brothers and the ranch away. Keeping busy helped, barely.

He spurred Prince on but suddenly pulled the reins hard to stop short as he stared at the open field in front of him.

"Sorry, Prince." He wrinkled his brow, glowering at the covered wagon on his property. Property that had been enclosed with a fence that should have warned strangers to stay out. Anger coursed through his body with great velocity. He was tired of people taking what was his.

He lifted his rifle out of the saddle scabbard and lay it across his lap as he slowly approached the camp. The aromas of smoke and coffee with a hint of bacon hung in the air. These folks were eating better than he. No time for cooking in his busy life.

He expected to see a few people, but the camp was silent. Did they have a gun beaded on him as he approached? He flicked his gaze to the side. They had damaged a good portion of his fence. Someone would have to pay. The urge to punch that someone mushroomed.

"Hello, the camp!" he hollered. Where were the thieves? Were they yellow-bellied cowards? He squinted against the sun, spotting movement near the broken fence. Was that a girl hand feeding one of his horses' grass? What the heck was going on?

"I'm coming in, and I have my rifle cocked!"

The wagon moved slightly. Someone was in there.

"Wait! Don't shoot!" a female voice called. Then, "Orla, where are you?" She sounded exasperated.

The woman quickly clambered out of the wagon. She didn't have a gun in her hands, but she might have one tucked in her skirt somewhere. Brogan kept his rifle pointed at her. Her big blue eyes grew even larger as her ebony hair blew in the slight breeze.

"Can I help you?" She clasped her shaking hands.

Frowning in confusion, Brogan scanned the camp. Where was her husband? She appeared too small and frightened to drive a covered wagon without one.

"For starters, you can tell me why in the name of heaven

you would take down my fence and let my horses loose." He pushed his hat back on his head. "Then I want to hear how you think you have the right to squat on this land." He narrowed his eyes. He wanted the truth the first time. It would be a nice change.

"What did you do with my sister? If you've harmed her…" With jerking, anxious movements, she scanned the area, darting quick looks from one end of the field to the other.

"I think that's her over there hand-feeding my horses," he snapped, as he pointed.

The woman put her hand over her mouth as her shoulders sagged and she released a sigh. She turned and stared at her sister. "Orla won't harm them." She returned her focus to Brogan. "My name is Ciara Doyle. The fence was already down, and it seemed safer to camp here rather than the wilds of Texas."

Wilds of Texas? "You'll have to move along. Don't think for a minute I believe you about the fence. Now if you'll excuse me, I have horses to find." He clenched his hands around his rifle and gave her a hard glare before he placed the rifle back in the scabbard. Brogan started to turn Prince but stopped. "Where's your husband?" He was still in the mood to punch someone.

"We don't have husbands," Ciara stated.

He fixed his gaze on her. "I'm to believe it's just you and your sister? Lady, I've been lied to by the best so don't bother. What's really going on here?"

Her chin quivered and she darted a glance at him before she began to shuffle her feet. "We were traveling with our parents, and now it's just me and my sister. We couldn't go on because the wagon train was too far ahead of us, so I turned around, and somehow… I ended up in Texas. I know it sounds like a tall tale, but I always go the wrong way. I have no sense of direction. I knew we were off course, so I decided since I always go the wrong way, I would go the other way instead, but that didn't help either. Pretty sure I wasn't supposed to cross that river about six days ago. I thought the west is on my left side and east was on my right no matter where I stood." Crimson seeped into her cheeks. "I have since realized I need to be facing north for that to work." When she looked at his face she winced.

He almost wanted to laugh, but he maintained the frown on his face. Who in the world would think everything left was west? It surprised him she didn't end up going in huge circles. It was crazy enough to be the truth, but that didn't make up for the fact that she was on his land.

"Where are you going from here? And since you didn't mean to go to Texas, where were you going in the first place?"

Orla walked over and took her sister's hand and gave him a childlike stare. She had the same blue eyes as her sister, but her hair was a golden blond.

"Is something wrong? You don't seem very happy, mister. I found a place that has some pretty flowers. Would you like me to show you?" She looked at him expectantly.

"Yes, there are lots of pretty flowers around," he said, struggling to keep his voice even. "But I don't have time for you to show me right now."

Orla tilted her head and her shoulders slumped. "Ciara is always too busy too. You have very nice horses. They come to visit every day. I like talking to them."

"You're joking, right?" As soon as he saw fear in her eyes, he was sorry. "What I meant to say was how many do you feed and where do you feed them? That, I have time to see, if you'd like to show me?"

Brogan glanced toward Ciara and watched as she smiled at Orla and put her arm around her shoulder.

"I think we should just leave. I can see we've made you

angry, and we don't want to trouble you. I'm sorry as can be about being on your land. But the fence was already down, and we didn't see any horses until that first evening. Orla talked to the horses, and the next thing we knew we were getting daily visits from horses which I assume are yours. If you wait here for a bit, I'm sure they'll come to you. Orla, you must pack up now."

Orla narrowed her eyes and gave him a big frown. "We have to go because of you, don't we? This is the best place we've been in a long, long, long time. We try and try to find safe places to sleep at night, and it's difficult. I point to a spot and Ciara will shake her head and say no. Then we have to ride in the wagon for a long time before she says yes. She wants to go back to St. Louis, and she'll find work." She tipped her head back and studied him. "Mister do you have any jobs?"

Ciara gave him a sad smile. "I'm sorry, we aren't asking you for jobs. We're capable of taking care of ourselves. Maybe you could just point me in the right direction. It shouldn't take long for us to pack up, and again I'm sorry."

He wasn't sure what was wrong with Orla, but she acted much younger than she was. She was sweet, and Ciara seemed decent enough, just wary, and weary. It was a long way to St. Louis, and they didn't have jobs lined up. They were bound to get themselves into a whole lotta trouble. But he couldn't offer them a place to stay. He just wanted to be alone. He refused to trust another person again. It wasn't like they were his responsibility…

He watched for a moment while Ciara started putting everything back into the wagon. She moved efficiently but some of the crates sitting outside seemed heavy. With a sigh, he swung down off Prince and began to help her. Their lack of supplies stunned him. What were they thinking? They wouldn't even make it out of the state of Texas. Sending them on might send them to their deaths. Panic set in; he didn't want anyone to rely on him. He could help them without getting involved. It should be easy enough. He'd take them to town and someone else could take care of them.

He whipped his head around at the sound of pounding hooves. Stepping away from the wagon his mouth fell slack in astonishment. From what he could tell, his whole herd was coming toward them. He'd never seen the like, and for a moment he didn't think they would stop. He raced toward Orla, ready to scoop her up and deposit her in the wagon but before he had a chance, the horses thundered to a halt in a cloud of dust.

But the horses didn't come up to him. They all waited for Orla to pat them on their noses. She'd somehow stolen his horses! They used to surround him like that, but now he was being ignored. Oh, the disloyalty of these horses… But the way Orla's laugh tinkled, calmed his jealousy. He'd never seen anyone so happy before, and it amazed him. What was it like to have a carefree moment to laugh in delight?

Brogan quietly walked to Ciara's side. "She sure has a way with horses. It's almost magical to watch. Has she always been that way?"

She gave him a rueful smile. "She was thrown from a horse when she was fourteen, and she has forever remained fourteen. Sometimes it's hard to look at her and know she's older than that. I expect she'll be living with me for the rest of our lives. Good thing I like her." She chuckled softly, and the sound washed over him, making him tingle as he lost himself in her blue eyes.

"Why don't I hitch your horses to your wagon and have you follow me to the house?" he found himself suggesting. "I bet the two of you could use a rest from the grueling traveling. I understand if you don't trust me. I trust no one either.

But I believe your story, and truthfully you don't have enough food to get much farther in your travels."

She looked pensive for a few minutes and then nodded. "Are you offering us jobs? We don't take charity. We work for what we have."

"There's always too much to do on a ranch, and I'm doing it on my own. So, any help would be welcome."

"All right, I accept." A smile broke over her face. "And thank you. We'll stay in the wagon. As soon as we've worked enough for the supplies we need, we'll get back on the trail." Her lips pulled into a pout. "I would've been back in St. Louis if there was a trail to follow."

He almost laughed, but he reined it in before it happened. Food; she probably cooked and cooked well. At least that was his hope. "I think we should set up a few ground rules. I'm off limits. I like being alone and I dislike chatter. That doesn't mean that you must avoid me. I'm just warning you I might avoid you. You need to know it has nothing to do with you."

Her smile returned. "We can respect your privacy. I'd best go tell Orla or I'll never get her away from the horses."

CHAPTER TWO

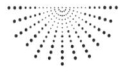

The house surprised her. It looked fairly new, but the barn seemed to have weathered many years. There wasn't much growing near the house, and somehow that made it look lonely. She pulled the wagon around to the back and stopped. It seemed like a good spot. There were oak trees that could provide them with shade and keep the scorching sun away.

"I can't believe we're living here. Ciara, I just love this house. Do you think I can have a room of my own?"

Ciara smiled at her sister. "We'll be staying in the wagon for a little while. Remember how we talked about being able to trust somebody and to never be alone with any man?" She waited for Orla to nod. "Brogan lives here alone. He seems very nice, but we don't know him. I'm sure as the days go by, we will find out if we can trust him or not. So, I'll say it again. I don't want you to be alone with him. If he tries to kiss you or touch you, I want you to let me know right away. I love you, Orla."

Orla gave her a warm smile before she hugged her. "I

know the rules to be safe. I love you too, Ciara. Do you think I could go into the barn to see more horses?"

"We have to remember that this is Brogan's ranch. If we want to do anything, we need to get his permission."

"You mean he's gonna be like our dad?"

Ciara's lips twitched, and she couldn't help but laugh when Brogan came out of the back door of his house. He looked to be at a loss for words and she took pity on him and stopped laughing.

"No, not like our dad. It's just always polite to ask first."

Orla mumbled as she shook her head, "Not allowed to do anything ever."

Ciara exchanged an amused glance with Brogan.

"I'm sure you will find plenty to do around here that will make you happy." Ciara grew serious. She would have to tell Brogan about the rule of not being alone with Orla. She understood, but she didn't understand at the same time and all it would take would be one slick cowboy to ruin Orla.

"Can I go to the barn?" Orla asked eagerly.

"Sure, you want me to take you down there?" Brogan asked.

"I have to go alone." Orla started making her way toward the barn.

His brow furrowed as he stared at Ciara. She felt the heat of his gaze as she watched Orla walking. She might as well tell him the rules.

"Orla's not allowed to be alone with any man. She looks like a woman, and a man would think she was a woman, but she's still a girl. I'm afraid for her. I'm afraid someone will take advantage of her so I've made the rule that she can't be alone with any man. I know it might seem strange to you, but it's the only way I know to protect my sister."

Brogan nodded. "I understand. It's a good rule. There are too many people out there who will take advantage of others.

And it's amazing how many people lie. I'll try to keep the rule in mind…" He sighed. "But it's not the biggest ranch."

"That was easier than I thought. Usually a man would say 'my ranch my rules.' You're different from others." She tipped her head to the side and studied him. "I'm not exactly sure how, but you are. In a good way." Her face flushed hot. She was babbling on like an empty-headed girl. "I'd be happy to make dinner if you'd show me the kitchen. Please let me know if I or Orla overstep boundaries you may have. It's difficult to get along with people you don't know. I just don't want us to be in the way. Oh, and one more thing, feel free to tell us to leave. I don't know if I'll be working here for a night or a week, but if you've had your fill, just let me know."

His eyes widened as he looked her up and down as though taking her measure. "A straight shooter. I like that. Come on, I'll show you the kitchen."

He led her through the back door and into the kitchen. The wooden floors weren't even marked up. The counters didn't have familiar knife marks, and the stove was one of the newer ones with the hot water reserve in the back. It was so clean she wondered if it had been used before. The shelves were loaded with dinnerware that didn't fit him at all. They were far from the tin plates she and her family had always used. But the yellow flowers on the plates were cheerful.

She walked over to the sink and was thrilled to see the indoor water pump. She had heard of them, but she'd never used one. "Do you have a root cellar?"

Brogan pointed to the floor. "It's right under there but it's empty. I have most of the food supplies stored over here." He walked to the closet, turned the knob and opened the door.

She'd seen nothing like it; a place for everything. It was a big closet, and she stood inside marveling at the selection of supplies he had. More heat rose into her face, and she glanced over her shoulder at him. "I shoved you out of the way, didn't I? My ma taught me to be a lady, and I'm sorry I pushed you."

He grinned at her showing his deep smile lines. He had probably smiled often before the war. He didn't seem to be much of a smiler now.

"Well I would call it more of a push than a shove. I don't know many women who would be so excited by a food closet. But considering how low your supplies are, I can understand. You and Orla are welcome to help yourself to whatever you want. I eat here or there." He ducked his head. "I don't know how to cook, so I eat beans out of a can. I do know how to roast meat, but only over an open fire."

"Well that is more than my father ever knew about cooking." Her eyes misted for a moment thinking of her father. She missed both of her parents so very much.

"Now, how is this supposed to work? Say Orla is in the barn, but I need to do something in there. What should I do?"

"Gently tell her she has to leave and just tell her it's the rule. She'll understand. It's been a bit of a trial always watching over my sister, but I love her so very much. She finds delight in the smallest things, and she always shares them with me. I just wish—oh, never mind."

"No, what were you going to say?" he prodded in a gentle tone. "You can talk to me. I don't have anyone to tell your secrets to."

She hesitated for a moment. *Why not?* "I wish that someday she would marry and have children of her own, but that will never happen. And I have found that most men won't marry me if she's part of the bargain."

Brogan tilted his head for a moment and frowned. "Men have said that to you? I don't see why it would be a hardship. Are you a mail-order bride? Is that why you were going West?"

It was her turn to smile. She had suggested being a mail-order bride, but her parents had been too upset about the idea. "No, there's no one waiting for me."

The door opened. "I'm always waiting for you, and I always will be," Orla said before she crossed the room and gave Ciara a hug.

After a moment, Orla let go and gazed at Ciara with great excitement in her eyes. "Come to the barn, Ciara! You must. There are baby horses with their mamas, and they have two cows. Imagine two cows! I saw a rooster, chickens, three pigs, and I even saw a goat with two little goats. Do you think the bigger goat is the mama goat?"

Ciara noticed Brogan's lips twitching. She was used to it, though, and it didn't make her laugh anymore. She just enjoyed Orla's excitement. "Two cows, you say? I think you'll have to show me after we cook supper. I have a few things I want to show you too. Come look. The water pump is inside." Both women went to the sink, and Orla laughed.

Ciara glanced at him over her shoulder.

He nodded and tipped his hat to her before he turned and went outside.

CHAPTER THREE

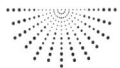

Brogan sat on the front porch and admired the night sky. Supper had been excellent, and now he sat listening to Ciara telling Orla all the reasons they had to sleep in the wagon. He finally understood how challenging it could be for Ciara.

Ciara had seemed to like the house, and he was glad. It surprised him their presence didn't annoy him. The house had been empty when he came, so he'd made most of the furniture himself. He'd always been good with wood. In essence, it was a brand-new home. He had looked for something that would've belonged to his mother but there had been nothing left inside the house. When Teagan's wife Gemma had lived here someone came and stole everything out of it.

A fresh start was good, though. It would've been better if the ranch wasn't next to his brothers' ranch. It didn't much matter he didn't fit in with them anyway. He'd always felt like an outsider and he knew that the woman who raised him loathed him. His father seemed to be wary of paying attention to him and it was because of that woman.

He'd been so angry when he first came here so disgusted with the lies and the betrayal. He hadn't cared if there was furniture in the house or not. In fact, he slept on the floor in front of the fireplace for about a month. Then he decided he didn't need the Kavanaghs. He had his own life to lead, and he couldn't wallow in despair. He'd set to getting horses and making furniture.

This was the first time he'd felt pride in his accomplishments, though. It was a strange feeling that warmed his whole body, and he was positive he'd never felt it before.

More words filtered over to him. He chuckled; Orla was now telling Ciara that she was not tired at all. She also informed Ciara that she wasn't in charge of her. And that sleeping was a personal preference. He couldn't help his chuckle from getting louder.

He stood and went back into the house turning off lamps all except the kitchen one by the back door. He'd leave this one in case they needed him. He glanced outside. Ciara was sitting on the ground with her knees pulled up to her chest and tears rolling down her face. He wavered. He wasn't going to get involved, but could he be of help if he let her talk about it?

No. Leaving her alone would be for the best. He glanced at her one more time, noted the shudders rippling through her body as she sobbed, and without thought he went outside, sat next to her and took her into his arms. She pulled away and stared up at him in shock, but he just drew her closer and stroked her back. It was surprisingly comfortable having a woman in his arms. But would any woman do?

He didn't know how to give or receive affection. He'd witnessed it plenty times but was never the recipient. His anger started to bubble inside, and he squashed it down. This wasn't about him; it was about a young woman with a disabled sister who had nowhere to go. Maybe he could build them their own house on the land? No, that wouldn't work. He'd have to ask Gemma's permission for something like that, and he was not about to ask for anything. She was his half-sister and owned the property, property that he should've had a share in. Both sides had shafted him.

Her sobs subsided, but he kept his arms around her. She smelled of vanilla, which surprised him. Holding her was a comfortable, warm feeling, one he'd never imagined. Were her sobs real or was she trying to make a fool of him? He shook his head, disgusted that he even had to think that way.

"Do you think you will be all right now?" He hoped she said yes. He needed to get out of there.

"Yes, yes I think so. Thank you. It's been a long time since I had a good cry. Don't worry, though, I don't cry every day." She gave him a sad smile as she stood. "Good night."

"Ouch!" Ciara shook her hand and then put her finger in her mouth. It was the second time she'd burned it while making coffee. She loved the stove, but there was a slight learning curve to getting it started and hot enough. She'd get it down though. She needed to.

That morning, Orla had shown her the sun's beautiful rays coming through the clouds. It had moved Ciara to tears. She didn't care what happened she would never be separated from her sister. She'd cried about it all night but she loved Orla. And taking care of her meant she needed a job. And that job meant she would need to master the use of the stove.

"Something smells good. I don't think I've ever had breakfast in this house before. Though I do enjoy a hot cup of coffee." Brogan bypassed all the pretty dinnerware, grabbed the one tin cup in the house and poured himself some coffee. "It's a treat to be greeted by two such beautiful women in the morning."

Orla laughed, and Ciara frowned.

"Did you hear what he said, Orla? That's what I mean by a sweet-talking man. They call you beautiful, and that's when you know you need to keep your guard up."

Brogan looked bewildered. "In all my years no one has ever mistaken me for a sweet-talking man." He took a sip of coffee and seemed startled to notice that Orla was staring at him. "Err… But your sister is right. It's good to be on the lookout for sweet talk." He turned to Ciara and gave her a boyish grin.

Did he even realize how sweet his grin was? He had said he thought of himself as a tough loner, but she wasn't so sure that's what he was. He seemed very sensitive to her. And… he'd probably be mad if he knew what she was thinking.

Brogan put his coffee cup down on the table, went to the hook by the front door and grabbed his hat. "I'll be in as soon as I milk the cows. It might take me a little longer since there are two."

"I'll wait awhile before I start cooking." She listened for the sound of the door opening and closing. When there was only silence, she turned to see what was going on, and Orla was standing next to him, whispering in his ear.

"What in tarnation is going on?" Ciara snapped. "Orla, come sit at the table and let Brogan get on with his work. He's a very busy man, and he doesn't have time for such foolishness."

Orla hung her head and dragged her feet to the table. Orla could be quite dramatic when she wanted to be.

Brogan glanced from Orla to her and then back to Orla again.

"Like I said, I'll wait awhile before I cook." She turned

back to the sink, and this time she heard the door open and close.

"I don't see why you're mad," Orla blurted. "I saw you and Brogan hugging last night. So, he must be a good man. You should allow me to go along with him. I know how to milk a cow. I could be a great help." She put her elbows on the table and held her cheeks in her hands with her lips forming the perfect pout.

"Orla, this is such a new situation, and I'm not sure what we should do or not do. I'm sorry I chastised you. I'm hoping this ranch will be a safe place for a few days. We'll need our rest if we're going to make it back to St. Louis before winter comes." She wiped her hands on a dishtowel and then went to Orla, putting her arm around her shoulders giving her a sideways hug. "If something ever happened to you, I'd be beside myself."

Orla nodded. "You'd be by yourself that's for sure. Can I milk the cow tomorrow?"

Ciara chuckled lightly. "You sure can be stubborn when you want something."

Orla must've taken it as a compliment because she smiled widely. "Do you think if I told him he's beautiful I can milk the cow?"

Ciara laughed again. "Now you're just teasing me."

"Yes I am. I'm eighteen, yet you treat me like I'm five. I heard you say I was fourteen in my head but even a fourteen-year-old could milk a cow. I thought we were supposed to help around here?"

What was Ciara supposed to say? Being overprotective came naturally to her now. Oh, how she missed her parents. They always were able to say the right things to Orla. Perhaps they didn't worry as much but Orla was all she had left.

After she finished her coffee, she got breakfast going. She

cooked the bacon and scrambled up some eggs hoping she had made enough. Once she knew where everything was, she'd make bread and biscuits. It wasn't long after she'd finished before Brogan came in carrying a pail of milk.

Orla jumped up from her seat and scurried over to him. "Can I go with you next time please, please? I want to help, but how can I help unless I drag Ciara everywhere with me? It would take more than one day to do a day's work if I had to do that. I already know how to milk cows so maybe you could go do something else in the morning."

"I'll be mending my fences today," said Brogan, shaking his head.

"Then that's what I want to do today! I want to fix fences." Orla smiled at Brogan.

"Orla, we've been through this already today."

Brogan gave Ciara an amused smile. "I think you *both* should come and fix the fence. The next time I believe you will think twice before you pull someone's fence down."

Ciara took a deep breath hoping it would be a calming breath, but it wasn't. He was a very hard man to read. His smile seemed to be one of teasing, but his words certainly weren't. What kind of game was he trying to play? She'd go, but she was bringing her pistol with her. Men weren't to be trusted.

Ciara and Orla washed the dishes and cleaned the kitchen before they went outside. They walked to the barn just in time to see Brogan leading out three saddled horses. She was glad to see the other two horses were smaller than the one he rode.

"You'll have to ride astride," he said in an apologetic voice. He let go of the horses' reins and all three went straight to Orla.

Ciara watched as Brogan stared at Orla. He seemed fascinated by her, and that wouldn't do.

"I think we should get going." Ciara grabbed the reins to one of the smaller horses.

"I wouldn't take that one," Orla said as she shook her head. "He said he would throw you. Now, the other one likes you."

There was no way she would get caught up in Orla's world of talking horses. She mounted the horse that supposedly said he would throw her and smiled in triumph at Orla.

Orla scrunched her face and shrugged her shoulders. "I'll get down to help you up when you're lying on the ground." Orla mounted the bay.

"See that, Prince?" Brogan asked his horse. "What do you think of all that?" Prince just gave him a hard stare. Brogan bolted onto his horse and rode.

Orla turned her horse to follow Brogan, and Ciara was not surprised that her horse seemed very calm and very easy-going. So much for Orla's ideas that he would throw her. After a bit, Ciara's thoughts drifted to the broken fence. What was she going to do to get Brogan to believe her? It made little sense. Why would they break the fence and not take any of the horses? They could have just as easily parked their wagon right on the other side of this fence. Maybe living alone made a person suspicious.

They rode for quite a while before they got to the broken fence. She swung down and watched Orla do the same. Before Brogan could say a word, the horses began to swarm Orla. Those horses were certainly taken with her. Ciara turned to Brogan and studied him while he once again stared at Orla.

"What do we do first?" Ciara asked.

"We need to dig a hole for the fence post. I also need to count the horses to be sure they're all inside before I enclose the pasture." He dug around in his saddlebag, pulled out a pair of gloves, and tossed them to her. "I wouldn't want your hands to get all callused and bloodied."

Ciara already had calluses, but she wasn't about to do anything that would make her hands bloody. "Perhaps I can just hold the fence post in place while you fix the fence?"

He gave her a slight nod. "Maybe you could count the horses for me while I dig this hole? I need an accurate count." He grabbed some of his tools and walked toward the space where the fence should be.

CHAPTER FOUR

*C*ounting horses should be easy enough. She'd start with the ones closest to Orla. At first, she had a good head count, but then the horses moved. To her, most horses looked alike. She could figure out the breeds or what they were bred for, but all brown horses looked identical to her. She counted five times and decided it was close enough. She wandered over to where Brogan was putting the wooden fence post into the hole he'd just dug.

He glanced up at her but didn't say a word. He looked sweaty, and maybe he was tired too.

"I've counted your horses, and you have thirty-nine."

"No, I don't. Go count them again." He turned his back toward her.

She jerked herself upright. He must be the rudest man in all of Texas. He had been so nice yesterday and last night, but today he was a different person. He was a prime example of a man who could not be trusted. She took a deep breath and strode over to the horses and began counting once again.

Each time she counted she got a different number. This

sure was not the job for her. She went back to Brogan. "You have forty-two horses." She turned and started to walk away.

"Wait, a minute. That's not the right number either. Are you sure you're actually counting the horses and not making up numbers?"

Ciara turned toward him and crossed her arms in front of her. Why couldn't he just give her a hint at what number he was hoping for? "How far am I off? I have counted and counted, but the horses keep moving."

Brogan took off his hat and started laughing. "Of course, the horses are moving. You didn't think they'd stand still so you could count them, did you?"

She wanted to stomp away, but that would be too childish. She wanted to hit him, but that wouldn't be very Christian, and neither would be calling him a few choice words. She gave him her best glare, but it didn't seem to faze him. She turned on the ball of her foot and marched off. He certainly was a fussy one, having to have the exact number. Too bad she didn't have paint with her so she could paint numbers on each horse.

"What is it you're trying to do?" Orla asked.

"I've counted and counted these horses so many times, but no matter what number I give to Brogan he says it's wrong. He even laughed at me. So, I'm counting them once again."

Orla wrinkled her nose. "There are exactly thirty-three horses. Why don't you ask Brogan if that's the right answer?"

"But how do you know?"

"Because I can count."

She turned and stalked to Brogan and gave him an artificial smile. "There are exactly thirty-three horses." She stared at him smugly, waiting for his answer.

"Orla told you, didn't she?" He roared. "You got the right number."

Ciara stepped forward and poked his chest with each word she spoke. "You are a bully, and you're not nice."

Brogan took a step back. He still laughed. "I don't think bullies are supposed to be nice."

She'd had all she could take. She had tried being nice and yet he just laughed at her. She deflated. Imagine, he got his amusement every time she failed. He had probably realized all along that Orla knew how many horses there were. But Ciara had tried and tried to count those horses to no avail and he stole her moment of triumph. She didn't need this it was time to go. Her eyes misted.

"You might as well leave the fence open for a few more hours so I can get our wagon through."

A startled expression fell over his face as he studied her. It was almost as if she was something very foreign to him. She'd been gently reared and almost never teased. Things were hard enough without someone trying to make another person feel bad.

"I don't want you to leave. You're mad at me, aren't you?"

"See those trees over there? I'll sit there and wait until you are done. After that, we will pack up and leave in the morning. I thank you for your hospitality." Her shoulders slumped and her walking slowed as she made her way to the trees. She sat down and leaned against the biggest trunk trying to keep herself together. She'd been a fool to think some of her burdens had been lifted off her shoulders by Brogan. He was right about one thing, though. They didn't have enough supplies to get out of Texas. She'd have to find a job where Orla could stay with her while she worked. She couldn't even think of a job that would allow Orla to be there. She shouldn't have gotten mad. She'd just made things so much harder for them.

She wasn't normally a crier, but these were not normal circumstances. She couldn't stop the flow of tears that ran down her face. She prayed for strength and she prayed for a safe journey. It was all her fault since she was the one that had gotten them lost. She couldn't even count horses right. There was only one thing she was exceptionally good at, making pies. Her breath caught. Maybe there was a bakery in town.

The horses still surrounded Orla. They must sense she wasn't capable of hurting anything. Her bright smile was a balm to Ciara's heart. Nothing should rattle her. She needed to be extra strong for Orla. God would provide, he always did.

CHAPTER FIVE

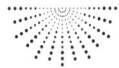

Brogan couldn't believe she called him a bully. He'd always been the one who was bullied by his… well it didn't matter anymore. He could tell by the way her shoulders shook she was crying and it was his doing. He wasn't sure what to say to her to make things right. He hadn't meant to, be a bully. He was having fun at her expense. She must be too serious.

He glanced at Orla. Ciara had a reason to be serious. An apology would be the best thing. He hadn't received many in his life though he wished he had. Now, how to go about it? It would have to wait. He was fixing the fence and he would not leave an open section for her wagon.

When he was done, he grabbed his canteen and took a long drink before he carried the canteen over to Orla.

"Thanks for the horse count."

Her eyes widened. "Why are you thanking me?" Her shoes seemed to hold some fascination for her.

"I'm going to bring water to Ciara. Will you be fine here?"

"I'm not a baby."

"I know." He couldn't think of anything else to say, so he walked through some tall grass to the trees.

She ignored him, pretending that she didn't see him. He sat down next to her under the tree, and still she didn't turn her head in his direction. He took off his hat and ran his fingers through his hair.

"I brought water."

There was no response from her. She must be the champion of the silent treatment.

"Listen, I'm very sorry I hurt you. I found it amusing, and it wasn't right. I'm used to nine brothers and we always joked around and wrestled. I'm not used to being around women and even though it doesn't seem like a good excuse… I'm not very good at apologizing. I am sorry I hurt you. It wasn't intentional. I feel horrible I made you cry. You have enough reasons to be upset, and I just made things worse."

"You didn't leave room for the wagon," she said with accusation in her voice.

He winced. "I don't want you to leave until I can get supplies for you. You'll starve."

She let out a heavy breath and looked out at the horizon. Then she straightened her back and turned to him. "I won't take charity. Let me know when I've earned enough for the supplies. It might take a month." She bit her lip.

"Two weeks tops, I bet. Enough time for you to get a rest and go over the map to St. Louis." He gave her a gentle smile.

"I don't know how to read a map. I can read, mind you. It's just that I've never even looked at a map. Will I be able to follow it and not get lost?" She shook her head. "My pa always drove the wagon so which way is west or east is a foreign concept to me. I never gave it any thought at all."

"It'll be good for you to know. Ranchers usually talk about places on their ranches in directional terms. Like the west pasture or move the cattle to the east. Sometimes right between morning and afternoon it can get confusing. Don't worry I'll help you."

A sigh burst from her, and a smile quivered to life on her lips. "And in exchange for everything I will keep house, cook, clean, do the wash and whatever else needs doing. Orla will keep insisting on milking one of the cows." Her smile widened. "Would you like breakfast before we all go to the barn in the mornings?"

He grinned. "You're a good person, Ciara. Which would Orla prefer?"

"She'd run to the barn in her night clothes if she could. I'll have the coffee ready and when we get back, I'll make breakfast. Does that sound good to you?"

"Yes, and I'll try to defer to you when she wants to do something, but she can be a bit slippery. Did she have your pa wrapped around her finger?"

Ciara smiled. "Oh, yes she did. Mother was forever being overruled. To my pa's credit he didn't know he was overruling my mother. My mother would just laugh and then tell Orla that what she did wasn't right. But since there was three of us one of us were always to be by her side. Now it's just me, and I can't go and do all the things she wants to do. She is my responsibility but not only that, I love her with my whole heart." She heaved a sigh. "I suppose we should head back. I bet everyone is hungry."

He stood and reached his hand out for her to take and when she did, intense feelings almost knocked him down. Quickly he helped her up and she looked as shaken as he felt. They both let go as soon as she was standing. They didn't glance at each other the whole walk over to the horses.

They rode to the house at a slower pace than when they'd ridden out. Finally, it came into sight. But as he turned to get Ciara's attention, he heard her scream. He whirled Prince around and spotted Ciara lying on the ground. Calling her name, he jumped down and ran to her. She sat up and peered around.

"Something spooked the horse," she claimed, glancing about.

"Are you hurt?" he asked as he kneeled next to her.

"Bruised probably, but other than that I feel fine." She gave him a distant smile, and he knew she hurt more than she let on.

He scooped her up into his arms and placed her behind Orla. "Hold on to your sister."

He started to walk to Prince when he heard Orla tell Ciara she'd told her the horse said he'd throw her. She could have been seriously hurt. Did Orla know why the horse had planned to unseat Ciara?

He grinned to himself as he mounted Prince. Orla had him believing she could talk to them.

CHAPTER SIX

A week later, Brogan sat on the front porch at dusk. He enjoyed having the Doyle sisters around. Orla was forever asking about ranching while Ciara made his house into a home. The week went by so quickly. He didn't want them to leave. It was a heart-filling feeling when he came home to Ciara and a home-cooked meal.

The front door opened. Glancing up he saw Ciara smiling at him. She was beautiful, yet she didn't seem to know it.

"Would you like more coffee or maybe more pie?"

His mouth watered, but he shook his head. "No, though another piece of pie is tempting."

She sat down on the edge of the wooden chair. "That's what I wanted to talk to you about." She wrung her hands for a moment. "I know a way I could earn money. I'd have to go to town of course."

"No."

She frowned. "What do you mean no? You haven't even heard me out."

"Go ahead so I can tell you I won't allow you to sell yourself for money." He was getting angry.

"Fiddlesticks, you have your mind on things you'll need to confess to God. Would it hurt to listen to a person before you said no?" Her shoulders slumped. She stood and went into the house.

He expected her to slam the door, but she didn't. Maybe he thought the worst of people. She hadn't done one thing that should make him assume selling herself was the reason she wanted to go to town. He rubbed his hand over his face. The nights were getting cooler, much cooler. It had to be cold in the wagon. He'd offered and offered for them to sleep inside. They could even share a room, but Ciara was firm in not accepting.

Now she had him wondering what she was going to say. Why would one want to go to town? His mind would just go on and on with ideas of what she might need to go to town for. He stood and strode inside then he stopped for a moment and slowed down. He didn't want to ruffle her feathers.

"Is Orla in the wagon already?" He hesitated at the pot then helped himself to a cup of coffee.

"Yes, she's sewing a surprise for you so don't disturb her." Her tone was snippy.

"I'm sorry for how I said no before you explained anything," he began. "There isn't much in town, and I jumped to conclusions. I don't know why I do it. Forgive me?"

"Maybe I'm too sensitive." She gave him a quick glance.

"No, you are not." He offered an apologetic smile. "I have a big mouth, and I don't give people the benefit of doubt. I feel as though I keep watching and waiting for some type of betrayal. It is not your fault. I'll try harder. I wish I could just stop these negative thoughts."

He sat down at the table across from her. "What I should have asked is what did you have planned. Especially since you looked excited."

She swallowed hard. "I've always won first place at any Founders Day or Independence Day celebration with my pies, and I thought I'd like to see if anyone would want to buy them. The general store or maybe at any restaurant? I'd need more baking supplies and you could take it out of my wages, what you said to me on the porch might very well be my fate in St. Louis. I just don't know. We might be here for more than another week."

"Your pies are very good," he agreed with a nod. "I don't see why not? You can make a few pies to give to the store owner or the restaurant owner. Once they taste them, I'm sure you'll get business. And… you can stay as long as you like. Just let me know when you want to go so I can free up some time."

The joy and excitement on her face was almost too much for him. No one had ever looked at him that way. She was drawing him in, and he couldn't help himself. He wanted nothing more than being wanted for who he was and not for who his family was.

"The only thing is, if we wait much longer to leave it'll be too late. It'll be bitter cold. Maybe Orla and I could rent a house or a room in town."

He wanted to scream no, but he waited a bit, calming himself. She was entitled to do anything she wanted. "You can look if you like, but wouldn't it be easier to just move into the house?"

She opened her mouth to speak and it was going to be a no, he just knew it.

"Just think about it," he interrupted before she could say it. "I have a very nice kitchen where you can make your pies. I could help deliver them if necessary. I hate to think of Orla closed up in a room in town. The horses will stop eating if she leaves, and skinny horses don't sell."

She burst out laughing. The sound rolled over him,

leaving warmth in its wake. She laughed for what seemed like a good long time. Finally, she stopped and caught her breath. "Brogan, I haven't laughed like that in such a very long time!" She stared at him with eyes that sparkled; beautiful eyes he couldn't pull his gaze from.

It would never work but he wanted this one moment of happiness. It flowed through him, and it was as though he tingled inside.

"You are a nice man, Brogan Kavanagh. I feel blessed I found your fallen fence to drive through." Her face turned a beautiful shade of crimson. She broke their stare and put both hands to her. "I feel strange. I will check on Orla."

He stood when she did and watched her leave. He tried, but the grin wouldn't leave his face. She seemed so honest, so genuine but he just couldn't. His grin faded and he banked the fire before he went to bed.

THE NEXT DAY Ciara was still trying to get the chill out of her bones as she made the coffee. Her shoulders tensed at the sound of Brogan's footsteps. She'd behaved like an ignorant schoolgirl last night. He had some strange power over her, and it was too unsettling. His grin was far worse than any sweet-talking she'd ever heard. It was downright dangerous.

"Yes!" Orla shouted as she ran to Brogan and hugged him.

"Did I miss something?" Brogan was grinning again with his laugh lines etched so deep.

"I'm moving in. I was so cold last night my knees knocked together all night."

"Orla, we don't mention body parts in front of men," she chastised.

Orla frowned. "You said I could treat him as I would a

brother. I never learned how to fish or climb trees." The gleam in her eyes had Ciara groaning.

Brogan turned to her. "Were your knees… I mean, were you cold too?" His lips twitched.

She lifted her chin. "I didn't have a moment of coldness. In fact, I never suffer such things."

He laughed. "Either you're cold or not. The other bedroom has two beds. The bedding is all new."

Orla ran by him.

"I'm getting the best bed!"

Brogan chuckled again, and Ciara stared at him. "There will be no more grins around here."

His brow furrowed. "What are you talking about?"

"I don't know but they have a strange effect on me, and I'd rather have my wits about me." Her eyes grew wider. "Stop laughing at me."

"Don't think I can. I'll go milk a cow or something." He was still laughing when he was outside.

She couldn't help her smile either. He was too dangerous. She'd said no to moving in, and now somehow, they were moving in. She sighed. She'd need to keep her guard up.

Brogan glanced up as the two women joined him in the barn. He peered around the cow. "I'm over here. Orla, did you want to milk Mercy?"

Orla was by his side instantly. "Oh yes. Mercy is a pretty name."

He grinned as he changed places with Orla. "It was the first I said to her. She kicked me and I said, ' have Mercy.' We've made our peace since then. She's friendly."

"I don't think she's listening to you."

Orla was whispering to Mercy and milking like crazy.

"My, goodness. You really know how to milk a cow. Orla, you're much faster than I am." Orla flashed him a smile and went back to her milking. "I'll go check on Bessie."

"Wait, I want to meet her. I'm almost done," Orla responded eagerly.

He met Ciara's gaze, and they exchanged grins. "I'll wait. You don't have to hurry."

He stood next to Ciara and he felt connected to her. There was something between them but as far as he was concerned, it was friendship and nothing else.

"You have a nice place, Brogan. You're a hard worker."

"I'm always busy, it seems, but it suits me. I get a real feeling of accomplishment when I see the horses. I've only been here a few months. I have a good herd and most of the mares have either foaled or are carrying. I have them in a separate pasture." He sidestepped putting a good amount of space between them. And he kept his gaze on Orla. She was moving on to the next cow with a fresh bucket.

They were moving in with him and he wanted to take the invitation back. He wasn't done feeling sorry for himself and he wasn't done with the hurt his family put upon him. He'd have to smile and he liked to do things when he wanted to. Regular meals were like keeping tabs on someone; expecting them to be there at a certain time. He wanted his freedom and they hadn't spent a night in the house yet.

"Brogan, do you think we could get a dog?" Orla asked.

He swallowed hard. "Only if you plan to take him with you when you go."

He saw Ciara stiffen out of the corner of his eye. He couldn't uninvite them.

"I'm going to get breakfast started."

"I thought you didn't want Orla alone with me." He tilted his head waiting for an answer.

She pinned him with a look. "I know you value honesty

and truth. I will trust you. Don't make me regret it." She turned and walked out of the barn.

She knew him better than he thought. It was a nice feeling to be trusted. He *could* be trusted. It was others he was wary of. Both had experienced life-changing events lately. He wasn't sure what he had done but Ciara didn't seem to be happy with him. If they would live together, he'd have to get to the bottom of it. There was nothing worse than living in a house with tension.

He watched in fascination as Orla talked to Bessie. Orla sure had a gift. A smile crept over his face, Ciara was probably mad that she had no choice but to move in to the house. He was learning through her frustrations that a body couldn't control everything. He'd be sure to knock off early enough to take her into town. Maybe when she was deep in pies, she'd be happier and more easy-going.

CHAPTER SEVEN

The trip to town wasn't going as Ciara had hoped. She was stuck in the middle on the wagon seat between Orla and Brogan. She could tell Brogan thought it funny to touch her knee with his. The first time it happened he apologized but the second time his lips twitched, and now he had the nerve to grin. She could see him from the corner of her eye, and he knew it. She didn't have any room to scoot over away from him.

She folded her hands on her lap and bowed her head. She wasn't prepared for games with a man. Why he thought it was funny, she did not understand. The only reason she could think was that he knew she felt something when he touched her. It was a rotten thing to do. He was a strange man. One minute he was caring and the next he was torturing her.

Best she think of something else. How many pies would the stove handle? Could she make enough to move her and Orla to town? Maybe with Orla's help she could manage it. Just the possibility that she wasn't stuck with Brogan made her heart lighter.

Orla chattered away and she stopped and stared at Ciara as if she was waiting for an answer. She hadn't been paying attention and that never sat well with Orla. "I think I see the town in the distance. What about you Orla?"

Orla set up straighter and peered into the distance. "It's bigger than I thought it would be! Still, it's smaller than St. Louis. Do you think the people will be nice? Do you think I could find a sweetheart? What about church? Is there a church? I bet they have one of those saloons I've heard about."

Ciara almost chastised Orla about the saloon remark but the look of surprise on Brogan's face was worth it.

"If you don't close your mouth, you'll end up with flies in it." She didn't even glance at him.

"What was that about saloons, Orla?" Brogan leaned forward so he could see Orla.

"I saw a woman once with the most beautiful hair and her lips were red. She had a shiny dress, something like I've never seen before. For a moment I thought maybe she was a princess but then I remembered there were no princesses around where we were. I asked my mother, but Mama told me to ask my father, and then he told me they worked at the saloon." She smiled. "Brogan, I would like you to escort me to the saloon."

Ciara had to bite her lip to keep from laughing. She would not say a word to help Brogan. He deserved it after all his knee touching.

"I would highly doubt your sister would approve of us going to a saloon. Isn't that right Ciara?" He gave her a sidelong glance.

"I told you I trust you with Orla." She pretended to be looking around as they arrived at the town. It was smaller than she'd thought. She wondered if there was more than one boardinghouse because she only saw one. The saloon was the biggest building and the dressmakers store was the tiniest. They drove by the doctor's office and Brogan stopped the wagon in front of the general store. She glanced in the other direction and saw what looked like a hotel. She hoped they had a restaurant.

Brogan helped Orla down from the wagon and then held his arms up to her. She hesitated and then he frowned. She didn't have a choice and the next thing she knew he had his hands around her waist as she held onto his arms. She let go of him much sooner than he let go of her.

Orla opened her mouth probably to ask about the saloon again, but Ciara spoke first.

"Let's go into the general store and see how much supplies would be to make the pies. Maybe the owner could sell a few in the store. Next, we should check with the hotel, and I'm sure there's somewhere else to eat around here too."

"You seem to have a good head for business," Brogan told her. "Not everyone looks at the cost to see if there will be a good profit." His eyes sparkled with appreciation and humor.

She refused to engage with him, striding ahead she opened the door herself. She waited for Orla before she started to look around. There was a big assortment of goods in the store.

She heard the bell over the door ring again, and there was Brogan. He was frowning. My, he was a big frowner. She'd have to ignore his frowns if she planned to get along with him. Was he like this with all people, or was it just her?

A tall balding man approached her. "Well, well it's nice to see a new face or two around here. I'm John O'Rourke, the owner of this fine establishment, and you are?"

Orla stuck her hand out. "I'm Orla Doyle and this is my sister Ciara. We live with Brogan and this is our first trip into town. It is a pleasure to meet you." She smiled at John as he shook her hand.

"Brogan!" he greeted. "Didn't see you there. Miss. Orla Doyle here has told me she and her sister live with you. That's an interesting development. Does the rest your family know?"

Brogan shook his head. "Nope."

John O'Rourke shrugged. "Well it's not their business anyway, is it? It's good to see you it's been a long time. Everything all right out at the ranch? I've heard tell someone's been rustling horses and cattle around here. Did they hit you too?"

"My fence was pulled down, but I think Orla and Ciara must've scared them off when they parked their wagon just inside of the opening. All my horses are accounted for, thankfully. They have any leads who it is?"

"From what I gather they don't have any suspects, and the animals they took aren't anywhere to be found. Keep a close eye on your herd." John turned to Ciara and smiled. "Now what can I do for you ladies today?"

Ciara got busy with the details of her pie making business. She asked John for a piece of paper and pencil and started writing down the numbers he quoted. She figured she could make a profit and if she saved enough well who knew.

Orla brought two ready-made capes to the counter. "I'd like these please."

Ciara shook her head. "We can't afford those. Orla, why don't you put those back where you got them?"

Orla made a face at her. "You know we've been so cold our knees were shaking."

"I'll buy them for you if you want them," Brogan offered.

"We'll be warm enough inside the house tonight." Her breath caught. Why had she said that? Flames of embarrassment licked at her face. She didn't like the questions in John O'Rourke's eyes. "We were traveling, and our parents died, so I turned us around, and then I got us lost. We've been staying in our wagon for weeks now, but the nights are getting cold."

"She means it's freezing in the wagon." Orla nodded.

Ciara didn't know what to say next. She didn't want to embarrass Brogan or bring him any trouble. She got the feeling the whole town would soon know she and Orla were living with Brogan. "We're cooking and cleaning for him in exchange for a place to stay."

"He lets me milk the cows," Orla said with great pride in her voice.

Brogan stepped forward. "Tell you what, John, we need to get a feel for how many pies people might take and then we'll be back with the list."

"Sounds like a fine idea. I'll see you folks it a bit."

Ciara's face was still on fire as she exited the store. She had a feeling anywhere she stopped Orla would make it sound as though they were living with Brogan. "Brogan, could you show Orla around town while I take care of business?" They exchanged knowing glances.

"I'd be happy to. Orla would you like to see the tearoom?"

"It would be my pleasure," Orla answered. "Right, Ciara?"

Ciara smiled and nodded. "I think it's a fine idea. I'll be back in a bit." She started walking down the boardwalk and went into every establishment that might serve food. There were butterflies in her stomach in anticipation of her success.

A short time later, she had orders for ten pies, and if the people liked them, there would be orders for even more. She scanned the street and didn't see Orla or Brogan. The tea shop would be her last stop. They weren't there, but she did get an order for two more pies. She walked back outside, wondering where they could've gotten to when she saw them coming out of the saloon.

Anger filled her. Orla was her responsibility, and she had done it all wrong again. She wasn't a good sister. She could barely take care of herself. How was she supposed to take care of Orla? It would have mortified her mother to know Orla had been in the saloon. What was Brogan thinking? She glared at him as they came closer.

"Are you all right, Orla? What were you doing in the saloon?" Ciara crossed her arms in front of her while she waited for an answer.

"Oh, you should have come with us. It's so beautiful. They have fancy chandeliers and so many mirrors, it was almost like a fairytale. It's a good thing Brogan followed me in there, because the man said I had to leave. No girls allowed. Why do men make up such rules? I just wanted to look, but unless I was going to buy some whiskey, I wasn't welcome."

That brought Ciara up short. "You could stay if you bought whiskey?"

"Let's go into the general store and get the supplies you need. How many pies will you be baking?" Brogan shepherded them toward the door.

"We'll talk about this later," she whispered. "I have orders for twelve pies. and that doesn't include the ones that John O'Rourke might be interested in. I promised them all apple pies this time. Do you have enough money to buy the supplies now and then I can pay you back? Twelve pies is a lot."

Brogan ushered them in and then smiled at John. "Do you have enough apples for about fifteen pies?"

"Hoo-we! That's a lot of pies. You did yourself well. I have plenty of apples. Ciara, why don't you come to the counter, then we'll figure how much you'll need of each ingredient."

"Put it on my tab," Brogan said.

Warmth like no other spread through her body. He really did care! Despite all the shenanigans, he cared. A thrill went through her. She smiled the whole time she was figuring out what she would need and how much.

"How are your brothers?" John asked. "Last I heard you weren't talking, but that was a long while ago. Your family and you must have made up by now."

Brogan said nothing, just glanced at John and then looked away. Maybe that was his answer? Ciara had not seen any brothers. She watched as John packaged everything up and piled the items into several crates. Brogan immediately grabbed a couple and went outside to put them in the wagon, and soon he came back in. He repeated this until he had all crates loaded. He didn't look like a happy man. Shadows of sorrow had appeared in his eyes. He came back in for one last crate.

"Thank you, John. It was nice seeing you again. Ciara and Orla, are you ready to go?"

They both nodded and thanked John O'Rourke before they left. Brogan set the crate in back and then helped them up onto the wagon. Ciara tried everything to get Orla to sit in the middle, but she refused. Taking a deep breath, Ciara sat down between them.

As they drove out of town, Orla asked several questions about Brogan's brothers, but she didn't get any answers. She heaved a sigh and just watched the scenery.

Ciara felt bad for him. It must be hard to break from family. She was trying to think of something to say when he started brushing his knee against hers again. This time she laughed. "What am I going to do with you? You have the best fun doing the strangest things."

"I don't find it so strange. In fact I find it—"

"There's no need to explain. I suppose you would do it to any woman sitting next to you." She inwardly cringed. Why had she made such a statement? Why had she brought it up in the first place? Was she flirting? This was flirting, wasn't it? Oh no, she wasn't the flirting type. Why had she done that? The question stayed on her mind the rest of the way home.

CHAPTER EIGHT

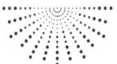

Why did everyone have to ask him about his brothers? They didn't know the story. They didn't know he was only a half-brother to the rest. Gemma had confirmed it when she looked at the family Bible. No one had looked at it in years. His mother, or rather Mrs. Kavanagh, had always had a special place for it on the mantle and didn't want anyone to touch it. He'd always thought because it was a family heirloom, but it was because they had added his name since his father was her husband.

Funny, he'd always felt her coolness and distance from him, always blamed her for her lack of love. But she hadn't asked to be saddled with another child. Especially one who was born to another woman. His father had thought the Kavanagh name special. Even in death, he proved it by keeping the ranch in Teagan's name only. He should have explained he didn't want the ranch cut up into pieces. It had hit Brogan hard since he never could please his father. His father's legacy, his ranch, was to stay whole. It made sense, but his father should have been the one to tell them.

And when he had found out about the deception… it had felt like another failure.

He fed the horses that were in stalls and glanced around the barn. Where was Orla? Hopefully, she wasn't catching too much grief from Ciara for going into the saloon. A soft chuckle slipped out. She sure was headstrong.

His mirth faded as he once again took in his surroundings. He needed to make enough money to buy the Maguire ranch from his half-sister, Gemma. She wouldn't want the money, but he needed the land deed to be in his name. He longed for something that belonged to just him. He wasn't ready to approach his family yet.

He often spotted one of his brothers riding the fence line looking for him. At least they knew where he was. Had Quinn come back? Quinn felt things deeply, but he loved them all. Yes, he'd be back.

Might as well go into the house to get his scolding for Orla going into the saloon. He grinned, Ciara's eyes flashed when she got mad, and he liked how she looked; so alive, so full of emotion. She made it easier to get out of bed in the mornings. He looked forward to seeing her.

When he stepped over the threshold, he inhaled deeply. The heavenly smell of apple pie filled the house. A smile lifted his lips, and his spirits rose. The two sisters were making the house into a home. But they didn't expect to nest for too long, did they? He closed his eyes. What did he want? He wanted to be alone, yet he wanted them to stay. But he wasn't ready to take a chance on people. Others had made him too big of a fool already.

"You two have been busy. Look at all the pies!" He meant the compliment with all his heart. But perhaps his enthusiasm would soften her chiding, too.

"There you are. Brogan, we need to talk about what happened in town," Ciara announced, her eyes flashing.

The sounds of plodding hooves and a wagon's creaking drew his attention to outside.

"It must wait. I hear a wagon pulling up." Word always spread faster than a horse with a racoon on its back. "It'll be someone from next door, I expect." His feet felt heavy as he shuffled back outside. Sure enough, it was Teagan and Gemma. His brother was married to his sister, and that struck him as strange. Teagan and Gemma had loved each other since forever. He wished he had taken the time to get to know her better. But the half-sister thing was sprung on him.

He braced himself for all kinds of questions as they drove up. He watched Teagan hop down and then lift Gemma to the ground. Gemma ran to Brogan and wrapped her arms around him.

"I'm so glad to see you! You've been missed very much."

Brogan pulled back, staring at her rounded abdomen in shock. "You're having a baby?"

She blushed prettily and nodded. "I want her to know her uncle."

Teagan put out his hand but hugged him instead. "He will want to know you. I think about you every day, but I didn't want to come over unless I was invited." He drew back and met Brogan's gaze. "Then we got the news, and seeing as Dolly was ready to take a parasol to you, I'd thought we'd best come over first."

"The news?" Brogan cocked his brow.

"Yes. We heard you've been entertaining two sisters and brought one to the saloon." He shook his head. "Brogan, the saloon?"

Brogan grinned. "That's right, and she had to leave since she didn't want to drink whiskey."

The door opened, and Ciara stood there, appearing upset. "Won't you come inside so we can explain?" She put her hand to her neck and didn't look up at them. Well, huh, she must have been listening through the door.

"Yes, come inside." Brogan urged. "There is nothing sordid going on."

Brogan told them the story as soon as everyone was seated except Ciara. She insisted on making coffee and bringing everyone a piece of pie. Finally, she was out of tasks and sat next to Brogan on the sofa.

"Oh, this is delicious!" Gemma exclaimed.

"My sister makes prize winning pies," Orla told them proudly.

"I want you to know that I am beyond sorry for putting Brogan in this position," Ciara began in an apologetic tone. "He doesn't want us here, not really. He says he does, but it's because he feels sorry for us. He has been so generous, and he has been a gentleman. We just moved into the house and only because we were so cold last night. We were brought up knowing right from wrong, to be ladies of high morals." She wrung her hands on her lap and her eyes looked moist.

"Don't," Brogan said. "We have done nothing wrong." He reached over and stilled her hands. "I don't care what people say."

She turned her head, and he knew she was crying.

Gemma sat forward in her chair. "We know nothing has been going on. Brogan is an honorable man. Brogan, you might not care but I'm sure Ciara and Orla would rather not be the topic of conversation in town. If they make their home in this area, they won't be respected. It's just the way it is and I'm sorry."

Teagan cleared his throat. "Brogan—"

"I know where this is going, and you can't tell me what to do anymore. I'm on my own and doing well." He allowed some heat into his tone. Anger filled him. Big brother Teagan to the rescue. Nothing ever changed.

"Brogan," Ciara whispered. "It's best we leave. I'm not used to hiding or sneaking around. You're right, we have done nothing wrong. But people will believe the worst. I have to leave, not for me but for the sake of Orla." She swallowed hard as she gazed at him. "We'll be fine. I know which way to go now, and we made it this far, didn't we?"

CHAPTER NINE

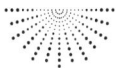

"Orla, we must repack the wagon. We might as well do it now."

Orla shook her head. "You can go, but I'm not. I don't care what you say, I'm not going with you. I'm staying with Brogan and helping with the horses!" She stood, lifted her hem an inch, and ran from the room. The front door slammed.

"Oh, no!" Ciara had tried to hide the fact she was crying, but there was no hiding it now. "Brogan, we need to go after her!"

He squeezed her hand. "She's going to the barn. She was so happy and now... I'm so sorry, Ciara. Everything that I think is right is wrong, and I had no business trying to help you when I can't even help myself." He gave his head a little disparaging shake. "I'm too jaded to be around people."

Gemma stood. "You could marry Ciara." Her pretty eyes were damp. If only she and her husband had never come over to Brogan's place.

"As nice as that suggestion sounds," began Ciara sadly. "Brogan will tell you he has no love to give. He wants to be alone, and I won't turn his life upside down because of gossip. It was nice to be off the trail for a while, but Orla and I need to push on." Ciara slipped her hand out of his grasp. She had known they wouldn't be staying indefinitely, and Brogan wanted nothing to do with her and Orla. He'd been very generous to them, but it was time to go. She stood straight and tall. "Thank you for coming to see us. It was very nice to meet you both." She hurried from the room. A sob bubbled up, and when she closed the back door, she slid down it and let that sob and the others that followed come.

She allowed herself a few minutes of crying before she picked herself back up and headed to the wagon. She'd have to take a good many crates out to repack the wagon. The weight needed to be even on all sides, and she had to be sure they were secure and wouldn't fly around while she drove. It was far too late to wish she'd allowed Brogan to buy the cloaks for them, but wish she did.

The wind picked up, and leaves drifted down from a few of the trees in a cascade of gold and orange. The rest of their belongings were in the house, and she had no wish to go inside just now. Brogan could take the pies she'd finished and sell them. After all, he had purchased the ingredients to make them. Hopefully he'd make a bit of a profit.

It was time to get Orla. Ciara's body tensed. It would be hard, and Orla would hate her. *Lord, help me explain so she understands. Help me maintain my dignity when I say goodbye and please keep us safe as we travel.*

Standing outside the barn, she heard Brogan explaining things to her, and he was giving her hope of building a horse ranch for herself. Ciara grit her teeth; there would be no more crying. She stepped inside. "Here you are, Orla. I have the wagon almost ready to go. I still have a few things we brought into the house to pack." She slightly turned her head to gaze at Brogan but it hurt too much, so she stared at some tack hanging on the wall behind him. "I'm hoping you can sell the pies. I didn't mean to leave with… I don't like leaving a job undone." The catch in her voice wasn't dignified, but it was the best she could muster. "Thank you."

She turned toward her sister. "Orla, it's time to go."

Orla ran to Brogan and wrapped her arms around him. "I'll miss you forever." Then she pulled back, turned and ran out of the barn. Ciara followed; she had no words to add.

They climbed onto their seats. Brogan didn't say a word; he just stared at her. This time she stared back, wanting to memorize his face. She cared for him, and her heart was tearing. The pain was almost too much to bear. Why had she let her guard down? Her dismay knew no bounds. She turned the horses and drove the wagon. She had the map he'd given her. When she got to the road her tears made rivulets down her face. There would never be another. She never wanted another. There simply couldn't be another.

The foolish hope she'd held in her heart that he'd stop them died when they halted to make camp. If he was going to come, he would have by now.

"Ciara, was he your young man?"

Taking a deep breath she gazed at Orla. "Now is not the time for anything like that. Brogan is a good friend. It seems unexpected things happened on this trip."

"Like Mama and Papa?"

"Yes, like that, but we made it through then and we'll make it through now. Let's get a fire built. It will be a cold night."

LATER THAT EVENING the sound of horse hooves broke the silence. Ciara's heart leaped, and joy filled her. He was coming to get them after all! She stood and waited by the fire with a smile on her face.

The rider wasn't Brogan instead it was John O'Rourke from the general store. "Howdy!" He swung down and tipped his hat to both her and Orla. "I have supplies for you. Brogan was insistent you get them." John took a big burlap sack off the giant bay along with his saddle bags. He placed the sack on their wagon's tailgate, and then he unloaded his saddle bags.

"He wanted you to have this too." He pulled an envelope from the front pocket of his coat and handed it to her.

Ciara looked inside and her heart dropped. It was money. She handed it back to John. "Please give this back to him. We were just travelers who happened upon his land, nothing more. Thank him for the supplies. Tell him that when I'm able to, I will pass along his lesson in generosity. It was nice to see you again, John."

"Best of luck to you both." He took his saddle bag and put it on his horse before he mounted up. She watched him ride away.

Her knees threatened to buckle and she quickly grabbed the tailgate and held on. She hadn't seen that coming. Her hopes were so crushed, she just stood there unable to think of what to do next. Orla stood next to her and started to put the items away.

"That was so nice of him, wasn't it?" Orla smiled.

"I'm tired. I guess it's time to go to bed," Ciara told her as she climbed into the wagon.

Soon enough Ciara stared at the canvas overhead. Sleep would have been a blessing, but it didn't seem to be coming. She hated to think of Brogan all alone until she remembered that he could have asked them to stay. He wasn't interested in a relationship, and he certainly didn't want her. She'd have to marry once they got to St. Louis. It was insane to think she'd find a job to support them. The weight of her situation dropped on her shoulders, and she didn't know if she'd ever be able to stand up straight and free again.

The only thing she had to hold on to was her faith. God was watching and keeping them safe. It had been more than a month since she buried her parents. She'd spent most of the time they traveled after that reassuring Orla. Brogan's place had given her time to fill her soul again. She'd been right about him. He was a nice man who never intended to allow anyone to get close to him.

But they had become close, and he must have known she cared for him. Well, he'd gotten his wish to be alone. But he'd also done right by them. The supplies were heaven sent, and she was grateful.

A shiver rippled through her. Brr, it was cold. She snuggled closer to Orla and felt warmer. She needed to rest. She needed to fall asleep.

BROGAN THOUGHT he'd be alone with the women gone, but it was quite the opposite. His brothers Sullivan and Donnell had taken it upon themselves to *help* him. He didn't need help. He wanted to work so hard and long that he'd fall asleep without thoughts of Ciara crowding his mind. He tried ordering them off the ranch, but they refused to go. He told them he had no brothers, and they ignored him.

Now he was reluctantly going to the Kavanagh ranch by order of Dolly. She had helped to raise them all, and with his parents dead, she was more of a mother to him. If Dolly wanted him to eat with the family, he'd go. It wouldn't bury the hurt that haunted his every day. The feeling of being betrayed would never leave.

He slowed Prince to a walk. The ranch land was in sight, and he needed a moment. He didn't want to talk about who his parents were. Didn't even want to think of them. His feelings were still too raw. Then the house came into view, and he winced. You'd think it was a Sunday with everyone looking nice and hanging around the front porch. The beautiful blonde must be Quinn's wife. He'd missed a lot. Sullivan had told Brogan about her.

He swung down, and the youngest brother, Shea hugged him and took the horse to the barn. He said nothing. What was he supposed to say? They would never understand anyway.

Dolly raced down the steps and hugged him tight as she laughed and cried. "My boy. Brogan, I missed you something awful." She took a step back. "Let me see you. What a handsome man you are!"

He grinned at her. He'd been gone months, not years. "I've missed you too, Dolly. Now I understand just how hard the work is you do. Laundry was the worst."

She laughed and took his hand then guided him up the stairs where he was hugged by Murphy, Fitzpatrick, Angus, and Rafferty. Gemma gave him a kiss on his cheek, and then Quinn squeezed the air out of him. He felt too stiff to hug them back.

"I'd like you to meet my wife Heaven and our children." Quinn's smile was the proudest he'd ever seen.

Heaven hugged him quickly. "This is Tim, Daisy, and Owen."

Brogan cocked his brow at Quinn for a second. "It's a pleasure to meet you all. Tim, don't let them work you too hard. Daisy, you are a delight. Owen, I bet Dolly just can't wait to get her hands on you each day."

"I'm a de… I'm a light," Daisy proudly informed everyone. She signaled with her finger for Brogan to bend down close and before he knew it she'd kissed his cheek. It was by far the most surprising and sweetest kiss of his life.

"Thank you, Daisy. Your kiss put a bit of joy in my heart. Very magical."

Daisy smiled widely and took his hand. "You can sit next to me."

"I thought it was my turn to sit next to you, Daisy," Donnell protested.

She giggled, but her attention remained on Brogan. "What games do you like to play? I like tag the best."

Tim took his other hand. "Do you fish? Fishing is my favorite.

Quinn was blessed. It was funny, because the last time he'd seen Quinn, his brother had hated women and now he had a wife and family.

They all took seats around the big dining table, and the women brought in the food. Teagan whispered something to Gemma, and she blushed.

They all held hands and Dolly thanked the Lord for bringing back all her lost lambs.

Brogan was mostly quiet during supper. He didn't want to be here. They never understood how hard it had been for him growing up.

"Unca Bro, can we see the lambs?" Daisy asked.

"I think you need to ask your pa."

She tilted her head. "You mean Dada?"

Brogan exchanged a smile with Quinn. "I mean Dada."

"It's good to see you smiling," Sullivan commented.

"I smile."

"Nope."

"Nope," Donnell echoed.

"Y'all need to see the horses Brogan has," Teagan told them. "He has a good eye for horseflesh, and he's great with them. Well, we already knew he had a knack for horses, but he's done a job he can be proud of."

Teagan's words chiseled away a piece of Brogan's frozen heart. No one had ever said they were proud of him before.

It had already been getting too sappy and uncomfortable in the house, and now the brother he looked up to the most had said he was proud.

"Horsies like me too," Daisy announced and then stared at Teagan. She started to stand up on her chair when Brogan took her and put her on his lap. She still stared at Teagan.

"Horsies do like you, Daisy. But we do remember that horses can be dangerous, right?"

She shook her head, her blond curls bobbing up and down.

"Daddy takes me with him. I ride on the horse with him," Tim boasted.

"That's why being the big brother is good. You're first in line," Brogan told him.

Teagan studied him, a thoughtful expression on his face, and Brogan immediately felt bad. "Teagan, I meant nothing by it. I got to ride before Sullivan and the other youngsters."

"If anyone should feel bad, it should be me. I had to wait until all of you wore our father out before I got a turn." Shae chuckled as he nodded his head.

Rafferty reached over and patted Shea's shoulder. "Poor baby."

After the plates had been cleared, Fitzpatrick and Angus volunteered to take the kids outside. Coffee was poured for the rest.

"Can I count on you for supper from now on?" Dolly asked Brogan.

He stiffened. When had one supper turned into all suppers? "I'm afraid not, Dolly. I can't make any promises."

She gave him an understanding smile. "But I can come there with food, can't I?" Her eyes widened as she stared at him.

"Sure, but I'm not there often. I'm out working with the horses. I have a few pregnant mares close to the barn, so don't anyone ride them." He turned his gaze on Quinn. "And I don't babysit, just so you know." He smiled what he hoped looked like a normal smile. Why wouldn't anyone let him be?

"Now, we must talk about the two women that lived with you. Your reputation has taken a bit of a downturn. Those poor women. You should have sent them to us," Dolly gently lectured.

He gaped at her and ran his fingers through his hair. "What exactly does a downturn mean?"

"Scoundrel and cad are being bandied around."

"That's just ridiculous. I did nothing wrong." He offered a half-hearted shrug. "Don't worry, it'll all die down."

Dolly looked skeptical. "Perhaps you're right. I just hope those poor girls aren't freezing to death."

Sullivan gave a slight nod in Dolly's direction. "It has been unseasonably cold out. I'm hoping it gets warmer for their sake."

Brogan's heart dropped. He'd sent supplies, but what good were supplies when people were freezing? He should have insisted that they stay or, like Dolly had said, he should've sent them over to the ranch. Why had he let them go? He'd missed Orla milking cows with him.

"I was thinking about that too. Ciara is very independent. I don't think she'd turn around and come back, even if I asked." He ran his hand over his jaw.

Gemma stood up and walked to Brogan. She put her hand lightly on the shoulder, and at her touch he gazed up at her. "Ciara cares for you. You didn't know that?"

"Sure, we got along, but that was the extent of it. No matter what, her plan is to go to St. Louis."

"If St. Louis is her dream, I hope they get there safely. It was nice of you to take them in." She let her hand drop and then sat back down next to her husband.

There was a long silence, and Brogan felt the need to squirm. He pushed back from the table and nodded to them all. "I need to get going. I have horses that need my attention." He stopped next to Dolly and kissed her on the cheek. "Thank you."

It felt strange to leave, knowing he was going to his own place. He still couldn't get over the fact that Quinn was married and had three kids. He wanted to know the whole story, but if Quinn wanted him to know he'd tell him at some point.

The moon was bright as he rode home, and only Prince's footfalls broke the hush of the night. Ciara would be looking at the same moon. How far in their journey would they be? Part of him wanted to say just forget it, and another part of him desperately wanted to go after them.

"Tarnation," he muttered as he reached home and reined Prince in.

He tied the horse to the hitching post in front of his house and hurried inside. This wasn't about what he wanted or didn't want. This was about them being safe and not freezing. He packed a few supplies and left a note on the table if anyone from the Kavanagh ranch came by. He went out and mounted Prince.

"I think we can make a good start. That moon is sure is bright, so we should be able to see at least for a few more hours."

CHAPTER TEN

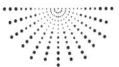

Orla and Ciara stood off to the side of the wagon, both wearing hopeless frowns. It had never occurred to Ciara that she'd need to know how to fix a wagon wheel. There'd been people on the wagon train that fixed wheels for others. Tears filled her eyes as she stared at the broken wheel.

She'd need to fix it and fast.

"That was the biggest rock ever. How could you not have seen it?" Orla crossed her arms in front of her and made a tsking noise.

"I have no idea, Orla, I just didn't see it. I hadn't been taking proper care of the wagon while it was sitting on Brogan's place. I should've known better, and I'm sorry. Oh honey, I just don't know what to do. Even if I knew how to fix or make a wheel, we wouldn't be able to lift the wagon to put the new wheel on." Ciara sank to the ground and looked up into the sky. *Please, Lord show me the way. Keep Orla safe. Thank you, God.*

"We could leave the wagon and take the two horses and

ride them. We're almost there, aren't we?" Orla sounded hopeful.

It was just as well she didn't know how dire their circumstances were. Maybe Orla was right, they could put some supplies on the horses and make their way back but instead of going to Brogan's they could go just a little farther and talk to Gemma. She seemed like a very nice woman, and she probably had good advice, at least Ciara hoped so. This whole trip from the very start had been doomed. Her pa had only wanted a better life for them, and now he and Mama were dead. If she didn't do something, if she didn't decide, she and Orla would be dead too.

"Orla, that was a great idea you had. I think we can put some supplies into smaller bags so we could load them up on the horses and make our way back the way we came."

Orla jumped up and down. "I knew we'd see Brogan again! I just knew it."

Ciara stood and went to the back of the wagon to see how to best consolidate what they would need. She had enough small flour sacks to pour supplies such as flour, sugar, and cornmeal each into their own sacks, and she would sew them up. She'd have to sew the bigger bags to keep the bugs out. They'd need water and everything they had that would keep them warm. Her heart sank. They didn't have saddles for the horses, and that was a big concern.

It took a bit of doing but Ciara had everything set to go. "Orla, could you please tell these two horses to be gentle? Explain to them we don't have saddles and I don't want to end up on the ground."

"I'd be happy to." Orla walked to the front of the wagon and talked to the horses. Ciara wasn't sure if she believed that Orla could make a difference, but she was desperate enough that it was worth a try.

She helped Orla onto one horse before she found a rock

big enough to stand on so she could get on the other. She'd have to be sure that when they stopped, she'd have some kind of mounting block nearby.

"Why do you look so sad, Ciara? You get to see Brogan again."

"Brogan doesn't like me, and that hurts my heart. I thought it better to never see him again but fate seems to have a different plan. The only thing we can do is make sure we survive the best we can and not worry. We'll find some help, I'm sure of it. Let's get going."

Orla was in the lead, since her horse seemed to listen to her. In fact, it looked like Orla was having a nice smooth ride while Ciara was being bumped around. It would be fine once they stopped for the night, she told herself. They didn't stop where they had stopped before because they made much better time than they did pulling the wagon.

"There seems to be a nice place ahead," Orla shouted over her shoulder. "I'll stop there, and you can tell me what you think."

As they pulled up, Ciara assessed the area. Orla had been right. It was a pretty place with plenty of water.

"Good job, Orla. You've been a big help today, and I'm proud of you." Ciara looked to the grass and didn't relish getting off the horse. Orla was already on the ground.

"Do you need some help?" It looked like Orla was smirking.

"Stay close in case I fall. I never realized how tall these horses were. How'd you get down anyway?"

"I just stepped on one of the bags we have hanging from the rope and then from there it was a small jump. Try it."

It was like a reversal of roles. Orla was the adult giving advice and Ciara was the child. She put her foot on one bag and then hopped down, stunned it was so easy.

First, they unloaded the horses then led them to water

and let them drink their fill. Next they hobbled them so they could graze on the plentiful grass. There was plenty of firewood around. It was quite a difference from when they stopped on the wagon train. The ground had always been picked over, and it was hard to find wood for a fire. The temperature dropped. Ciara made the fire while Orla got the coffee ready to boil.

"I was thinking about making some flapjacks. If I make enough, we can have them tomorrow for breakfast and the noon meal. What do you think?" Ciara didn't wait for an answer, just described the supplies she would need and started to mix up the batter. As she prepared the flapjacks, she couldn't help but wonder what had happened to the wagon train they had been on. If it was this cold in Texas what must it be like crossing the mountains? She glanced over at her sister. Orla seemed to be getting too close to the fire; she must be frozen. "Why don't you grab some of the blankets and we can sit on them instead of the cold ground?"

When the flapjacks were done, they both huddled near the fire with their coffee and their food. The fire made a big difference. Orla's face wasn't as bright red as it had been. The sun was setting and hopefully the moon would be as bright as it was last night.

She hadn't been paying attention, and she should have. The next thing she heard was a man's voice.

"Hello! I hope I'm welcome to share your fire." He was an older man with a white beard and shaggy white hair. His coat was missing the all the buttons, and his stained trousers had holes in them.

Oh dear. He was terrifying. Where was the gun? She should always keep the gun with her . How stupid could she be? She was supposed to protect Orla. Fear washed over her as Orla grabbed her hand and squeezed it.

The man was coming, whether or not she welcomed his presence. She gave him a slight smile. "Where are you from?"

The man looked all around before he sat down. "Oh, I'm from here and there. Mostly where I can find a job. What are you two lovely ladies doing out here?"

Where is that gun? That was all that was going through Ciara's mind. The man's squinty eyes never seemed to leave Orla's face. Orla must have noticed too; she squeezed Ciara's hand again. "Let me check and see if we have an extra cup." It was hard pulling her hand out of Orla's grasp, but Ciara stood. She started to walk toward the supplies, thankfully spotting the gun.

She heard a rifle being cocked and whirled around to face the stranger.

"Now don't be going and doing anything stupid. If you run or pull a gun, I'll kill her. Your best bet would be to come back and sit down."

A shiver went through her, and she couldn't breathe, but she took a step and then another toward the fire. "I thought this was a friendly visit." She held her voice hard and even.

"It'll still be friendly." A leering grin slid over his face. "You just might not like my definition of friendly. Tell me about yourselves."

Ciara sank down next to Orla, who immediately grabbed her hand again.

"It wasn't a suggestion. Tell me about yourselves." If there was a voice of evil, it was his.

Ciara took a deep breath. "Our wagon wheel broke, so we are on our way back where we came from. There's a town not too far away from here, and I'm hoping someone there can help us. In fact, I bet we'll see people riding by soon."

"People riding by soon was a good one." His harsh chuckle made her skin crawl. "There ain't nobody out here.

There's just the two of you and me. Now, I'd like some coffee."

Ciara started to stand.

"Not you. I want the other girl to get me the coffee and get me food."

Orla's face was stark white, and her hand shook. Her eyes grew wide, and Ciara could see the terror in them. But she stood poured coffee into her cup and handed it to him. Then she took her empty plate and filled it with flapjacks. She put her fork on the plate and tried to hand it to him stretching her arms as far as they would go, keeping herself away from him.

The man laughed. "Come sit next to me, darlin'."

Orla frantically shook her head. "I don't talk to any sweet-talking man." She marched back to where she'd been sitting and sat back down.

Ciara waited for the man to complain about Orla, but he didn't say a word. He looked at her as if he was studying her for a moment before he ate.

"The name is Elmer. What great luck I'm having, finding the two of you. Too bad you don't have your wagon, so you can each have your privacy."

What did he mean? Privacy in general or was he talking about something sinister? Sinister, she decided, he was sinister. Somehow, she had to get to the gun and keep them both safe at the same time. She tried to relax and keep her face expressionless. After she accomplished that, she'd try to smile. Maybe she could lull him into thinking they were helpless. "I'm Ciara, and this is my sister Orla." Usually she would have said it's nice to meet you, but that wasn't the case. How were they going to get out of this one?

He finished his meal and slurped the last of his coffee, and then he looked at both of them for a bit before he gazed at Orla with a glint in his eyes. "Either of you married?"

"No mister, we're not," Orla told him in a loud steady voice. She sat up straight and glared at him. "I think it's time for you to go, Elmer. It's easier to travel while it's still light out."

Ciara wondered how Orla had become so brave. And she was concerned that Orla would anger the man. She glanced around, looking for Elmer's horse. There was no sign of one, but that didn't mean there wasn't one hidden somewhere. It was too cold for this man to be out wandering around. What was he doing here?

"I'm not going anywhere. I like it right where I am. We'll be having a good time together later. Right now I'm so full I can hardly move, but don't be fooled into thinking I can't shoot you. Though I like the spunky one." He stared right at Orla.

The two women exchanged terrified glances. Ciara was frightened for Orla; it was never a good thing when the bad guy liked a woman. Maybe when it got dark, she could hit him over the head with a piece of wood. He'd have to go behind the bushes at some point, wouldn't he? They could get on the horses and be away in a flash. No, it would take too long to unhobble the horses and get on them. There must be something she could do, though. She was responsible for Orla, and she'd rather die than allow that foul man to take Orla from her.

"I can see you're thinking, and I know what you're thinking. There's no way to escape except if you call death an escape. I want *her*." He nodded toward Orla. "You look to be too much of a thinker. Thinking just gets women in trouble."

Beside her, Orla shuddered, and Ciara wished there was something she could to. She reached over to grab a few more blankets.

"What you reaching for girl? I'll shoot that hand right off. Don't think I won't."

"Orla's shaking and it's getting colder. I was reaching for blankets." Fear enveloped her as Elmer stood. He aimed his gun at her and then threw a long piece of rope to Orla.

"Orla I want you to take that rope and tie your sister's hands behind her back. Maybe it'll keep her from getting into trouble and making me kill her."

It was as though Orla was frozen with fright. She didn't move, but she made a couple of sounds of distress. Ciara elbowed her, and she seemed to come out of whatever daze she was in. She stood and caught the rope Elmer tossed to her.

"Nice and tight. If it's not tight, I will tie you up too."

Orla did what she was told, and she made those ropes tight. *Oh, Orla,* thought Ciara in dismay. How was she supposed to get out of these knots? She tried to sit as still as possible. She didn't want to make this hard on her sister; it wasn't her fault at all.

"Now put a couple blankets around her and then wrap them in place with the rest of the rope. I'll make the final knot after I check your work."

All he was doing was making Orla shake harder. This time when Ciara and Orla gazed at each other, it was if they were conveying their love for each other. They both knew the danger they were in, and it broke Ciara's heart.

Elmer plodded over and examined Orla's work. He smiled and nodded, and then he made the final knot in the rope. He seemed pleased with himself. Ciara hated him even more.

"Grab the rest of the blankets; we can use them."

There had to be something Ciara could do. But she couldn't move and didn't have a single idea. She waited for Elmer to instruct Orla to lay the blankets down but he didn't. Instead he added more wood to the fire put a rope around

Orla's wrist and then walked away with her running behind him to keep up.

Ciara was stunned. She was so angry, and tears flowed down her face. Harshly, she blinked them back. She didn't have time for tears, only had time for action. She looked around and decided that maybe she could loosen her bonds by rubbing the rope against the hard bark of the tree behind her. She started to move when she felt something under her leg and paused. It was hard and cold, but it was taking too long to move enough to see what it was. There was no more patience left in her body, so she wiggled and gave one final jerk to the side. Finally after frustration and more frustration she saw a knife. Orla's knife! Their father taught them how to defend themselves, but she didn't know that Orla still carried the knife. It was another few minutes before she could grab it, and then it was forever before she sawed through.

CHAPTER ELEVEN

*E*xhaustion plagued both Brogan and Prince. They had traveled most of the night, but now clouds covered the brightness of the moon. Why couldn't he just lie down and sleep instead of having to build a fire to make sure he didn't freeze to death? He got down from his horse and dropped the reins, knowing Prince would follow him as he gathered firewood.

After grabbing what he could find, he set the kindling on the ground to light it. But he paused as he caught what might be the flicker of fire in the distance. It was pretty far away, but he couldn't take the chance that he might miss Ciara and Orla.

He climbed back on his horse. "We'll go slow, Prince, I promise."

He rode half the time and walked the other half. He needed to be sure that Prince didn't step into any gopher holes. Weaving through the woods, using the trees for cover, he made his way to the site. Finally, he got close enough to see it was just one woman sitting by the fire, but he couldn't tell what she was doing. Why would a woman be out here alone? Brogan crept forward, leading Prince, and when Ciara came into view, he almost fell over.

He ran the rest of the way to her. She was wild-eyed and didn't acknowledge him at first.

"Ciara, it's me, it's Brogan." He repeated the words two more times before he took her hands in his. She started fighting, getting a few hard blows in. He stepped back and stood with his hands on his knees, trying to catch his breath. "What happened? Where's Orla?"

She looked at him in a strange way and tilted her head one way and then the other. "Brogan?" She didn't wait for an answer; she rushed at him and wrapped her arms around his middle.

He pulled her tight to him and held her. She trembled from head to toe. Whatever had happened, it must have been bad. Gently, he led her to the blankets near the fire and sat her down. He sat next to her and rubbed her arms trying to warm her.

Pulling away, she shook her head. "We don't have time. Brogan, we need to go. Orla is out there. We might find her before that man…"

Brogan stilled. "What man?"

"His name is Elmer, and he walked up to our fire trying to act as though he was nice. The next thing I knew I was tied up and he was hauling Orla away with him."

"Did they ride double on the man's horse?"

She shook her head. "I didn't see a horse, but I'm sure he must've had one somewhere. He tied Orla's hands in front of her and started walking and poor Orla had to run to keep up with him."

Brogan frowned as his stomach churned. "How long ago was this? Do you know?"

"I'm not sure. It took some time for me to cut the rope. I'd say maybe a couple of hours." She stopped trembling and stared at him. "Let's go get my sister."

He glanced around and realized there was no wagon. The horses were there but not the wagon. He turned and cupped her cheek with his hand and turned her face a bit so she was looking at him. "What happened to the wagon? Did he take it?"

Ciara took a deep breath and let it out. "No. The wheel broke, and I didn't know how to fix it. We had no choice but to take what supplies we could carry and ride the horses back the way we came. We thought we'd maybe be welcome at the Kavanagh ranch."

Brogan let go of her and looked up at the sky. The clouds were dispersing; maybe they could set out. It hurt that she said they had been traveling to the Kavanagh ranch and not his. He thought she had feelings for him but he'd been mistaken.

"Which way do they go? Will you be all right staying here? Do you have a gun?"

"That way, I'm coming with you, and my gun is around here somewhere. I'm not staying alone. Who knows how many *Elmers* are out there? I can ride one of the other horses."

He stood and helped her up. "Find your gun and wrap a few blankets around yourself. It will be faster if we ride double. You don't weigh much more than a bird. He thinks you're tied up, so I don't think he went too far, at least not for the night. I don't know who this man is. I've never heard of anyone named Elmer in these parts. Prince can't go any farther right now. Let me just put the saddle on one of the other horses, and we can head off."

She got busy looking for her gun. When he finished saddling the horse, she was right there waiting for him. He mounted up and then held out his hand. "Put your foot in the stirrup so you can mount up behind me. Then I want you to wrap your arms around me and don't let go." She made it in one try.

He turned the horse around, and they started in the direction Ciara had last seen Orla. It was dark and slow going. They made progress when the clouds passed, but there were plenty more clouds floating toward the moon. Not far from the sisters' camp, the two sets of footprints became one and a horse's hoofprints began. It was incredibly hard to keep his body from tensing up. He didn't want Ciara to know just how worried he was. More than likely Elmer was one of those trapper type men that lived alone. He probably planned to keep Orla for good. They stopped and waited for the clouds to pass, and then they started again. This was all his fault. He should've insisted that they stay.

"I will get off the horse so I can see if I can find the tracks. They were visible before, but I think they turned off somewhere near here." He swung her down and then dismounted. "Just stay where you are. Don't walk around."

Her silent nod worried him.

Once again, he had to wait for the clouds to pass, but as soon as they did, the moonlight showed him the way. "They turned through the bushes here," he whispered. He put his finger to his lips to signal for her to be quiet. "They might be camped close to here. We will walk very, slowly."

She nodded, and it was a relief to see she understood him. He grabbed his rifle and turned. He was glad to see Ciara had her gun out. After several slow, very slow, steps, he stopped and she ran into him, but she remained quiet. He pointed toward a fire and made eye contact with her. He didn't want to get any closer until he knew what was going on. He wanted to make sure it was just Elmer and Orla, and they hadn't met up with anyone else. Orla looked to be scared but intact. Her clothes were torn, though. She kept looking around into the dark while Elmer made the mistake of staring into the fire. Orla would be able to see them when they made their move, but Elmer would have to wait till his eyes adjusted to the dark. Elmer must think he was safe.

Making no sound, Brogan inched them closer, so they'd come up behind Elmer's back. His rifle lay on the ground, and Brogan wondered what was going on. Every man knew not to stare into the fire, and they also knew to keep their rifle across their lap. They watched Elmer put some tobacco in a pipe then light it and smoke it. He was talking to Orla, but they couldn't hear what he was saying. It couldn't have been very nice from her expression.

Brogan had never been so proud. Orla saw him, her gaze meeting his stare, but she didn't give him away. He half expected her to smile and wave. Brogan snuck up on the other man until he had his rifle pressed against Elmer's back.

Elmer rounded on him, his eyes squinting as he struggled to focus. He was still in a sitting position, not giving him any advantage at all. Ciara leveled her gun on the man.

"I should just shoot you down for the dog you are. But I must attend to Orla." Ciara lowered her gun and went to the other side of the fire where Orla was quaking under her blankets.

Orla burst into tears and snuggled against Ciara, who quickly twined her arms around her sister. "I thought I'd never see you again, and that was the saddest thing ever."

"Ciara, want to help me tie up this sorry excuse for a human being?" asked Brogan.

Ciara smiled and gave a little chuckle. "I know from experience that Orla is very good at tying someone up."

Orla touched her hands to her face, which was turning a bright red. "I only did it because he told me to. But I must admit I am very good at it." She jumped to her feet, grabbed some rope from the ground, and cautiously walked around the fire. She actually smiled as she was tying Elmer's hands behind him.

"I could've given you a good life, girl. Just think of how we would've been together in my cabin."

"I have a life of my own thank you very much. Plus you stink. Your clothes stink, your breath stinks, everything about you stinks!"

Brogan stroked his jaw trying to hide the fact that he was smiling. But one look at the gleam in Elmer's eyes when he looked at Orla turned that smile into a big old frown. They had a couple choices here. They could keep going until they got to the wagon and he could fix the wheel for them, or he could take them back home. No, Ciara said they were headed to the Kavanagh ranch. She hadn't said a word about stopping at his place. He didn't know why, but that didn't sit right with him.

He gazed at Ciara and realized he didn't want to take her back to her wagon. He didn't want to fix her wagon wheel. He wanted her to come with him to his home. But how was he going to convince her that that was a good idea? She was a good woman, and she'd been up front about everything. She wasn't a liar or cheat. In fact, she was the most generous woman he knew. And she was right. She'd have a hard time finding a husband who would take Orla in too. He didn't mind, though, because he liked Orla. Plus Orla made Ciara happy. And he enjoyed having their company. Both of them.

"Are you going to stare at Ciara all night, or are we going to make a plan? Personally, I'm all for leaving Elmer tied up. He did the same to Ciara and then told me how the wolves would eat her up. He's a ghastly man." Elmer started to protest her idea of leaving him, and she simply took her handkerchief and stuffed it in his mouth.

"He told you that. He said the wolves would eat your sister?" He turned to Elmer and kicked him in the leg. "What kind of monster are you?" Brogan shook his head in disgust. "Keep an eye on him, Ciara, and if he moves shoot him."

Prince wandered into camp, having followed at a slower pace. Brogan took Prince's reins then led him over to a tree nearby and let him graze. After a bit, Prince was all set, and Brogan grabbed the coffee pot from his saddlebag. He walked over to the spring and filled the pot with water. One part of him was livid and the other part was relieved and still yet another part worried. The best bet would be to hunker down by the fire until morning and then head home.

Now to convince Ciara that it was a good plan.

"You ain't gonna shoot me," Elmer sneered. "I bet you don't even know how to shoot that thing. Two girls traveling on their own, you were asking for trouble. Any man of worth would've refused to let you go. If I were you, I wouldn't go back with that guy. Seems to me he let you go once, so who knows what he'd do next time?"

Orla hit him on the shoulder. "I'm going to tie the handkerchief so it stays in your mouth."

Ciara thought it was just a threat until Orla pushed the cloth back into Elmer's mouth and then used a length of rope and tied it around his head. Ciara couldn't help it; she started to laugh.

"You're not laughing at me are you, Ciara?"

"No, of course not. Well maybe just a little. I love that you seem to know how to deal with this awful man, and you tying the rope between his teeth and around his head seems funny."

Orla smiled a proud smile. She stood up, gave Elmer a nasty look, and hurried over to where Ciara was sitting. "I could practice my shooting now, don't you think? Elmer could be the target." Both women burst out laughing when Elmer's eyes grew wide in fright.

When the laughter stopped Ciara took both of Orla hands into hers. "He didn't touch you did he? Did he try to…"

"Of course not, but if you hadn't come, he would've done what he wanted to. Oh Ciara, I was so scared. He had a horse waiting when we left from our camp, and he threw me up in the saddle so I was laying over facedown. The whole time I was trying not to be sick. It didn't seem to me we went very far before he stopped here. He mentioned something about having me tonight and you tomorrow… so long as wolves didn't eat you. I kept trying to think of ways to get away from him, but there was never an opportunity. Ciara, I just want to go home."

Ciara glanced up and met Brogan's concerned gaze. She watched him put the coffee on to boil before she answered Orla. "I'm not sure where home is but we will make one as soon as we can. I believe Gemma will be happy to have us stay with her for a while. We can help Dolly. And as soon as the nights aren't as cold, we can make a plan where we want to settle. I promise you by this time next year we will have a home."

Orla hugged her and held onto her tight. "I like your plan. I enjoy sleeping in a house because I like to be warm."

"Well, I think we have one more night to get through, and tomorrow, if we push it, we just might make it to the Kavanagh ranch before dusk. So why don't we gather the blankets and make the beds so we can get some shut eye?"

Brogan's gaze turned troubled, and she wondered what was on his mind. They wouldn't have a chance to talk privately, at least not tonight. She wanted to tell him how grateful she was that he cared enough to come after them. But *why* had he come after them when he had been free to be as alone as he wanted to be?

Ciara helped Orla pile a few blankets on the ground, with a few left to lay over them. They made two beds, one for her and Orla and one for Brogan. Brogan took one blanket and draped it around Elmer. Elmer tried to sputter, and Orla gave him a look of triumph.

Brogan poured coffee for them, and they drank the hot liquid before they lay down on the blankets. Then he helped to tuck them in. His eyes seemed probing when he looked at Ciara, and she wasn't sure why. Then he lay down so his head was near hers.

"Are you warm enough?"

His question warmed her heart, and she nodded.

"Maybe we should add more wood to the fire so we don't have to worry about it. I don't think we'll be sleeping more than a couple hours anyway."

She closed her eyes and listened while he put two more logs onto the fire and then while he got into bed and pulled his blankets up around him.

Sharing Orla's body heat kept her nice and warm and knowing Brogan was close enough for her to touch made her feel safe. She felt herself starting to drift off when Elmer starting making as much noise as he could.

"I could tie you to one of the trees over there if you like," Brogan warned.

Elmer quieted for a time it was if he was waiting for them to all fall asleep for him to make noise again. He kicked the coffee pot and there was a loud clang as the pot flew into the air. Orla screamed and they all sat up. Elmer had slowly made his way to their side of the fire.

"That's it. I gave you a chance and I warned you, and now here come the consequences. Ciara will you hold the rifle while I escort Elmer here to one tree? If he breaks loose, don't be afraid to shoot."

"I'd be happy to help."

She took the rifle and held it on Elmer as Brogan untied the man's feet, helped him up and took him over to the tree where he tied him again. Brogan looked grouchy as he returned and got into bed.

"Did you want your rifle back?"

"Yes, could you hand it to me?" Ciara handed the firearm over and snuggled with Orla again. She didn't enjoy having to treat people badly, but there wasn't anything else they could do. Elmer was dangerous.

The next morning, Brogan had everyone ready to go back to Ciara and Orla's camp. They found Elmer's horse a pretty paint tied not far away. Brogan put both Orla and Ciara on Prince and then he put Elmer on the paint facedown while he took the horse without a saddle. When they reached the camp after just a short journey, they discovered all of their supplies were still there, including their other horse.

Ciara stared at the fire. It had gone out. How long ago had it gone out? She would have frozen to death if not for Brogan.

Brogan got the fire roaring while she made more flapjacks. They were hungry, and flapjacks were filling. They cleaned everything up and organize the supplies. This time they each had their own horse as they headed back toward the Kavanagh ranch.

CHAPTER TWELVE

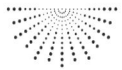

They rode at a decent pace, and at one point, Brogan pulled Prince up right next to her horse.

"Why do you want to go to the Kavanagh's instead of mine?"

"You made it clear you didn't want us there. Us being there is scandalous, and I just—I don't have the energy to be somewhere that we're not wanted. I just think it will be easier to go to the Kavanagh ranch."

"Is that how I made you feel?" he asked softly. "I made you feel unwanted. Sometimes I think I'm the biggest idiot in all of Texas. It was lonely with you and Orla gone. Sullivan and Donnell took it upon themselves to come help me work. Those two can talk and talk and talk. I think you'd be happy to know I even had supper with the family."

"You did?" A sense of delight filled her. "How did you feel? What did you say? Were they happy to see you? Oh, I wish I could have seen you there."

"At first it felt odd." He shrugged. "Everyone was hugging me, talking to me. But by the time we finished supper, it wasn't so bad. I had blamed them for all the secrets, but recently I realized they weren't the ones keeping the secrets initially. And Teagan, well, he didn't make out the will, and he didn't want us all leaving. He knows that he should've told us, but he made the best decision he knew how to." A smile crept over his face. "Teagan told me he was proud of me when he heard about my horses. No one's ever told me that before. It was like having a wound that had been festering being washed and bandaged."

She was so happy for him she felt she might burst. Maybe he could get on with his life in peace without thinking there was another betrayal just around the corner. His smile was different now; it seemed more carefree and made him look even more handsome than before.

He was obviously aware that having her and Orla stay at his place would change everything. His family would insist that he marry her, and he wasn't ready for that; she didn't know if he ever would be. And she refused to be in a relationship where she loved but wasn't loved back. Oh, he liked her; she could tell that now. But *like* was miles and miles away from love.

HOURS LATER, they were riding up to the Kavanagh house. Ciara's thighs were in so much pain she wasn't sure she'd be able to stand when she got on the ground. Orla was happy enough, but Brogan… he was preoccupied about something. She tried to talk to him, but he didn't want to talk to her. She was glad she'd decided not to stay at Brogan's ranch. Sullivan and Donnell were there to help her and Orla off their horses. She had to hold on to Sullivan longer than she intended. Heat seeped into her cheeks; she knew how it looked. Well, maybe she didn't, but it must look worse than she thought as Brogan looked ready to kill.

"Let's get you two ladies inside and get you warm," Sullivan said.

Ciara tried to take a step and almost fell. Sullivan quickly lifted her up into his arms and carried her inside the house. Her face grew hotter still, and Sullivan gave her a knowing grin. Exactly what that grin meant, she was uncertain. It sure would not be easy to live with all the brothers. It was a relief when Sullivan finally put her down.

Orla walked inside on her own accord. She seemed very proud of her achievement. "Ciara, I told you to relax more while you're on the horse. When you tense all your muscles, that's when they end up hurting." Orla took a seat on the couch next to Ciara.

An older woman came running in, wiping her hands on a dish towel. This had to be Dolly; she looked just as Brogan had once described her. "Oh my, what happened? I was so worried when you two left." She looked them both over. "You both look fine as far as I can see. Do I need to bandage anything? I'm Dolly," she finished, confirming Ciara's guess.

It was so nice to have someone who cared. "We're both fine, and it's good to meet you, Dolly. I'd get up, but my legs don't want to work after being on the horse all day."

"It sure is good to be back here, Dolly." Orla bounced on the sofa when she talked.

"Well I can at least get you a cup of coffee and something to eat. Don't worry, I'll bring it to you. I know what it feels like to be on a horse all day." She glanced around. "I take it Brogan's with you?"

Ciara nodded.

"Then I'll wait until everyone's here so you only have to tell your story once." Dolly turned and briskly walked back into the kitchen.

"It's warm in here and feels so good, doesn't it, Ciara? I'd rather stay at Brogan's, but this is fine. And I like Dolly." Orla smiled, but there was still a bit of terror in her eyes. "Where's Elmer?"

The sound of cowboy boots on the wooden floor let them know they weren't alone. Ciara would've turned around, but she just didn't have the energy.

"Orla, I have two men taking Elmer to the sheriff in town. You won't have to worry about him again. I know it might take you a while to get over what happened, but we're here for you."

Dolly stood at the door, and her eyes widened as she hurried to put down the coffee and a plate of cookies. "Who is Elmer, and what did he do to Orla?" Dolly put her hands on her hips, glaring at Brogan as though it was his fault.

"It's a long story, and like you said, we'll just tell it once, but Orla is fine and she wasn't touched." Ciara said, as she and Dolly exchanged glances of relief.

"In that case, let's get you warm and fed." Dolly bustled around until she had the coffee poured and everyone had a cookie, including Brogan, Sullivan, and Donnell.

Ciara shivered and wrapped her arms around her middle. They were lucky and they were blessed.

Brogan got up and put another log on the fire. He grabbed two quilts and placed one on Orla first. When he went to lay the other over Ciara, he seemed to be taking extra time. Their gazes caught, and he looked at her intensely. A thrill raced through her whole body, and she wished she knew the ways of men. Well not their ways, exactly, but what each grin or the looks in their eyes meant. He broke off the locked gaze first and looked around as though he didn't realize other people were in the room. His face tinged pink as he sat down and picked up his coffee cup.

BROGAN COULDN'T GET ENOUGH of Ciara. He knew he was staring, but he couldn't help it. It was as though there was a war going on inside of him. Part of them thought he should stay away from her, and the other part wanted to get closer. He'd have to leave her be until all of him wanted to be closer to her. He didn't even know who he was anymore, and he didn't want to be the type of man who changed his mind about how he felt. He'd given Ciara too much hope with the way he was with her and that had to stop.

She'd been wise to make them come to the Kavanagh ranch instead of his. In his home, she would have been far too much of a temptation. Her lips were a berry color, and they looked plump and ripe to him. How he wanted to hold her close and kiss her. To taste those lips. It would be hard, but he would have to avoid her; that was the only way to keep her safe from him. Women weren't to be trifled with.

Orla went into the kitchen to help prepare the supper. He could hear her chattering to Dolly. Orla sure had much more gumption than he had given her credit for. He had been worried she would react before they were ready when they had first arrived at Elmer's camp. But she had been brave and kept calm. He wouldn't have imagined that she could stuff a handkerchief into Elmer's mouth and then tie it in place with rope. She was much braver than she thought.

One by one, the whole family gathered and made room around the big dining table. Everyone wanted to know of their adventure, but it wasn't an adventure at all. So much could've gone wrong and he could've lost Ciara for good.

Orla was the one who told the story. She did a mighty fine job and left nothing out. When she told them about the handkerchief, Brogan couldn't help but laugh. That story would stay with her for a while, no doubt. She laughed with him.

"I can't believe I did that either. But thanks to Brogan. He was a true hero." Orla cast her gaze around the room and smiled. Tim had switched seats with Donnell so he could sit next Orla. He hung on her every word.

"Wow, a real live bad guy. Do you think he's an outlaw? Do you think there's a wanted poster for him? You think he's in jail yet?"

"Tim, let Orla eat. You can ask your questions later," Quinn told him.

With a reluctant nod, Tim started to eat his supper.

Daisy stood on her chair and put her hands on her hips and smiled at everyone. "I think Orla is a hero. She is very smart." She gave them all another smile and after a little curtsy, she sat down to eat.

Brogan watched as Quinn and Heaven smiled at each other. It was so obvious that they were in love and that was what Brogan wanted and nothing less.

"If it's fine with the rest of you, Ciara and Orla would like to stay here for a while. I'd take them to my place, but you were right, it wouldn't look respectable."

Teagan smiled at him as though Brogan had just won some prize. "Of course, they can stay. We were hoping they'd stay before they left the first time. We have more than enough room, and they are both welcome."

Tears ran down Ciara's face, and she dabbed at them with her napkin. "Thank you," she croaked out.

It tore at Brogan to see her cry. He wanted to comfort her. He wanted to hold her in his arms and tell her everything would be fine, but he didn't have the right.

"I'm sorry I'm crying at the table. It's all been so overwhelming, and your kindness went right to my heart."

"No need to apologize," Gemma said with a smile. "It happens to all of us."

Dolly began to clear the table, and Gemma and Heaven

both jumped up to help. "You girls sit down. Ciara could you help me in the kitchen for a moment please?"

Ciara was slow in getting up, and she groaned. "Dolly, I'd be more than happy to help you."

As soon as Ciara and Dolly were in the kitchen, everyone exchanged surprised expressions.

"She probably just wants to make sure Ciara is fine," Sullivan said.

Donnell nodded his head in agreement.

Yes… that must be it. Brogan sat back and relaxed. Ciara was tough, and she was fine—a little shook up but fine. He'd have to make a plan for him and a couple of his brothers to go get the wagon. He would bet Ciara and Orla didn't even have a change of clothes with them.

"Do you think Dolly is mad at Ciara?" Orla whispered.

"I don't think so. It takes a lot to get Dolly mad," Donnell whispered back.

Orla nodded slowly as if she was taking in Donnell's words and thinking about them. "Brogan will you tell the horses I said hello and I'll be visiting? I don't want them to forget me. Or… I could come over there and talk to the horses myself. I'd have to bring Ciara along. Would that be a problem?"

Brogan grinned. "I don't see a problem with that at all."

He waited for Ciara to come back out of the kitchen. He wanted to know what Dolly said, but Ciara didn't tell him. However, he *was* enlisted to help carry water for Ciara and Orla to bathe in.

It was harder than he thought it would be to say good night and then leave. He wished he had his old room back, but those days were past. Now he was a man with a ranch to run.

CHAPTER THIRTEEN

The next day Ciara sat on the front porch drinking coffee and watching the sun come up. It was a spectacular site with all the oranges, yellows, pinks, and purples sweeping across the horizon. Her thighs still hurt from riding the horse, but she'd be fine in a day or two, and she was determined to pull her weight. Dolly liked the idea of her baking pies, but she'd have to make them over at Brogan's because the oven here seemed to always be in use. It was perfectly understandable. Brogan would work anyway, so it wouldn't be as if they'd run into each other all the time.

It had been stupid for her to leave when the weather was so cold. She had put Orla in grave danger, and for that she couldn't forgive herself. She knew now she had just expected too much of Brogan. He might not even have it in him to love. He'd never shown love before to any woman, at least as far as Dolly knew. The conversation she'd had with Dolly in the kitchen had been nice and also illuminating. There was no reason to wear her heart out on Brogan.

Dolly had suggested she let Brogan lead things if he would. He was interested, and Dolly could see he cared, but she didn't want Ciara to get hurt. Not a lot of sleep had happened last night, as Ciara's mind had refused to stop whirling with her thoughts. Dolly was right, but what she didn't know was that it was too late. Ciara already loved Brogan.

But she could bake pies at Brogan's house. She wouldn't have to see him every day, and if he came over, she could be occupied with something somewhere else. She'd tell Orla she would be allowed to go to Brogan's without her. They both trusted Brogan. She heard the others get up from the table and go out the back door to start their day. Gingerly, she stood and slowly walked toward the kitchen to help clean up.

There weren't as many at the table that morning. Quinn had a house of his own, and about half the brothers ate at the bunkhouse because it was quicker. Orla had smiled throughout breakfast; she must enjoy their company. They were very nice men, but to her one was missing and she'd have to get used to it.

She was just about to ask Dolly what else needed to be done when she heard a wagon pull up, and a peek through the kitchen window revealed that it was her wagon. Someone must have gotten up early to get it fixed. She stepped outside, and her heart bounded with joy when she saw that it was Brogan.

"How'd you get the wagon here so fast?"

Brogan tied up the reins and climbed down. He smiled at her as he walked up the steps. "I couldn't sleep, so Prince and I along with your two horses went down the road, and there was your wagon. I fixed the wheel hitched up the horses and here we are. I figured you can use your clothes."

"Your hard work is much appreciated. I was just about to ask Dolly what I should do today, but I see now I'll be busy unpacking the wagon."

"I could stay and help if you like."

"No. No you have enough to do it your own ranch. If I can't lift something, your brothers are all here. I won't try to do more than I can. Would you like a cup of coffee before you leave?"

His eyes brightened for a moment, but he shook his head. "You're right, I need to get back. Tell Orla I asked about her. Have a good day." He untied Prince from the back of the wagon, mounted the horse, and set off.

Ciara rubbed the back of her neck trying to make some sense of their exchange. It appeared they were both of the same mind. They shouldn't get involved. Her heart dropped, but she knew it was for the best. At least she had gotten to see him today.

A WEEK LATER, Brogan was wrestling with the same fence that he had just fixed. He thought he had done a good job on it last time, but the boards were all loose again. He was growing tired of being by himself. He missed his conversations with Ciara. Was she doing well over at the Kavanagh ranch? Did she even miss him? He took off his hat and slapped it against his thigh. It was worse to know she was near and they never saw each other.

He didn't need anyone, right? After all, he was a loner. Being a loner wasn't much fun, though, when there was no hate to feed on. He wondered what God would think of all this. He would be glad about the forgiveness. But what about the thoughts Brogan was having of holding Ciara in his arms? He didn't know.

He was already on his knees he might as well pray.

Dear Lord, I'm not even sure what I want to say. I mean You already know everything. I need some help. I need Your help. How do I learn to trust someone completely? I've forgiven my brothers and I have forgiven my parents, but how do I know that Ciara would never lie to me or betray me? She hasn't yet, but I feel like I'm waiting to catch her in a lie so I can be happy and say I knew it and walk away from it all. That would be a big mistake, wouldn't it? Help me see my path. Help me change and learn how to trust. Thank You.

Just saying it aloud made him realize that it wouldn't only be a mistake, it would ruin his life. He had to make sure she stayed. It was time to visit the Kavanagh ranch and remind Ciara about the pies. Hopefully, that would work.

He rode Prince to the Kavanagh house, and as he passed the barn, he thought he heard Ciara's voice. Orla's voice would've been expected but not Ciara's. He climbed down, patted Prince on his neck, and pretended to be strolling toward the barn.

He walked in, and no one was in sight. But Ciara's voice could be heard again. Continuing to the end of the barn, he opened the stall and stared.

"What are you doing? We hire people to do that. Did someone tell you this was your job now?" He gritted his teeth. There she stood in an old dress with a shovel in her hand.

"What? Oh this. I volunteered because I had nothing else to do and I like to keep busy. I've mucked out plenty of stalls in my life. Just because I'm a woman doesn't mean that I can't do anything on this ranch." Her eyes burned bright and then dulled.

"Come, take a break with me, and I'll show you the stream." He held out his hand to her and when she put hers in it, he felt something he had never felt before. It went much deeper than just wanting to hold her. He wanted to know all about her. He wanted to be her best friend. He could tell by how her eyes widened that she felt something too.

They left the barn holding hands and walked across the

meadow until they got to the creek. It was his favorite place, the place he went when he needed to think. The bubbling of the water flowing down over rocks, combined with the rustle of the leaves blowing in the wind, soothed him. He'd hear an occasional bird or crickets, but otherwise it was very peaceful. He led her to a large rock that was flat then lifted her up so she could sit on it. Quickly, he scurried up next to her.

"You never told me about the wagon train and why you didn't go with them after your parents died."

She was silent for a moment, and then she turned to him. "Orla and I took the time to bury our parents. So many people were sick, but the train had to keep going. It couldn't stop for anyone. I guess we stayed longer than I thought because we traveled the whole day and never saw the wagon train again. Orla and I were heartsick, and we decided to turn around and go back to what we knew instead of moving on ahead alone."

A frown creased his forehead. "They didn't send any scouts to look for you?"

"They talked a great deal about how we were leaving so late in the season, but everyone was willing to take the chance. So they just left us behind. They told us they wouldn't have time to come back and search for us. I didn't expect them to."

He took her hands into his again, and this time he kissed the backs of both. "I'm sorrier than I can say. I don't know how you did it. With the sorrow from losing your parents, and the belief that you were alone... plus you had Orla to take care of. That's a lot. I don't even think you know how strong you are. I admire your strength and determination because it's mixed with much kindness." He gazed into the distance for a moment, then sought her eyes again. "I have a confession to make. I've been trying to come up with ideas about how to get you over to my place so we could talk and I could see you again."

She chuckled. "And tell me what excuse you decided on?"

He grinned, cautiously thrilled at her response. "I decided to go with the pies needed to be made. And if that didn't work, I was going to tell Orla the horses needed her and you. I know Orla would have come along and dragged you with her."

"I was going to use the pie excuse. I told myself that you'd be busy and I wouldn't be a bother. I decided I probably wouldn't even see you, but it would have been worth it if I had just glimpsed you. You became part of my life, and I missed you. Leaving your place was one of the hardest things I've ever had to do, but it seemed to be the right decision."

"I know you're Christian, but do you believe? Do you really believe?" he asked. "I've been praying a lot lately for God to show me my path. It's taken a lot of faith to believe that there is even a path for me. But having faith has filled my heart in a different way. It makes me want to throw out the bitterness and let all the good things in. I don't know if I'm explaining it very well, but before this I had decided to stay away from you. I was convinced that you would either lie to me or betray me because that was what I was used to. And I knew I couldn't go through it again. But you're neither a liar nor a betrayer. You're full of kindness and generosity, and it opened my eyes to what I might miss if I let you go." He glanced away, not wanting to see her face. He'd been too open, too honest, too vulnerable.

A shudder rippled through her. "I've been telling myself to avoid you at all costs, because you will tear my heart out. You had love inside of you, but you had too much bitterness to let it out. I was elated when you said that you had forgiven your brothers and your parents, and I hoped to see another side of you, but I didn't see much of you after that. Dolly said

I'd wear out my heart on you, and I knew she was right. I had told myself the same thing. I wanted to be near you, but it was so hard being near you and not being able to see you. I've never felt this way about anyone else before, and I've been wishing my mother was still alive so I could ask her if this is what love feels like." She drew a deep breath. "It also scared me, and that's why I packed the wagon and left. But you have to know I'm a package deal. It's not just me, it's Orla too. If you can't accept Orla as a constant in our life, then we must say goodbye here and now." Her brow furrowed as if she was waiting for him to say no to Orla.

He shook his head, bemused. "I've known from the beginning that you were a package deal. It's fine for Orla to live with us for the rest of her life. She's gifted with animals, and she has a sweet and kind nature." A chuckle slipped out. "Plus I think my horses miss her."

Ciara's soft laughter made his skin tingle.

"I want to tell you everything about me," he went on. "My father and Gemma's mother had an affair, and the result was me. Mr. Maguire wasn't about to raise me, so as soon as I was born he dropped me off here at the ranch. The woman I knew as my mother couldn't stand the sight of me, though I grew up never understanding why. I was never good enough, and I received no hugs from her. The worst was I could see her affection for my brothers. My father didn't bother with me much. I swear I worked harder and longer than anyone, yet I couldn't win his approval. I found out the truth about six months ago, and I couldn't stay. To top it off, my father left the ranch to Teagan. It was Teagan who explained later that it was so the ranch wouldn't get divided up or parts sold off. But it all overwhelmed me and fed into my feelings of being unwanted and unlovable. I became a classic loner." A smile tugged at his lips, and he let it form. "But you changed everything for me. You opened my heart, and even though I didn't want to feel anything, I was able to let most of my anger out. I feel more at peace now. I prayed on it too. I never thought any woman would take a second look at me."

He shifted until their gazes met. "You did. I still can't believe I let you go. I never wanted you to leave. It was as if my heart was doing somersaults when I was near you. And I *was* afraid of my feelings at first, but now I welcome them. God helped me to open my heart. I think you are beautiful and brave and the best sister to Orla that she could ever have. I admire so much about you, and I'm taking a big chance here telling you this… but I love you."

So many expressions crossed her face, and his gut began to hurt. "We should head back." His good mood faded, and he couldn't even summon the smallest smile for her. He slid off the rock and lifted her down. When he started to pull away, Ciara wrapped her arms around his neck.

"I love you too," she whispered. Her smile grew and her voice strengthened. "I have for a while now, and I'm so glad your heart was unburdened and you have room in it for me. I tried not to love you for Orla's sake. But I know you care for her too. You are the handsomest, smartest man I know. You work hard, and I see how you gaze at the children. You'll make a good father. I want to be with you every day."

He gave her a quick kiss and grasped her hand, leading her back to the house.

CHAPTER FOURTEEN

Their carefree moment had passed and now doubts filled her. Shortly after they'd professed their love for one another, Brogan had left with no explanation. Ciara's heart physically hurt, and she didn't want anyone to know. Had she scared him off by telling him she wanted to spend every day with him?

For the last three days, Orla had begged to go see the horses, and Ciara was at the very end of her rope. Everyone had stared at her at one time or another, and she only wanted to be alone. She needed to lick her wounds and make a plan for her and Orla.

Watching the huge snowflakes fall saddened her. They wouldn't be able to leave until spring. Snow or not, it was still too cold at night. Nothing would ever come of her pie business. It was as though one by one she'd had to let her dreams go until they were all gone. Maybe it was for the best. Dreams only caused her grief. She had responsibilities, and that would be her life now. She'd dreamed of children too. Shaking her head, she grabbed a cloth and began to dust.

Too bad dusting didn't take much thought. She put the

cloth down and went up to the room she shared with Orla while her sister was in the barn brushing horses. Ciara lay across the bed and wept into her pillow. She just didn't understand.

Are you there God? Of course You are. Forgive me for even asking. Thank You for opening Brogan's heart. I bet it's made a big difference in his life. Thank You for giving Orla and me a warm place to be. She has such a gift with animals. But I'm at a loss. I've tried so hard to be a good woman, and I've tried even harder to be a good sister and an example for Orla. I suppose that's my calling, to keep Orla safe.

She was far better off than most, and here she was crying. She just needed to buck up and forget about Brogan—or any man for that matter. She got off the bed and washed her face. She still looked as though she'd been crying, but there was no help for it.

Ciara wandered downstairs. The dusting had all been done. She followed the voices in the kitchen and came upon Dolly and Gemma. "I'm sorry," she said. "I didn't mean to shirk any of the work."

Dolly hurried and put her arm around her. "Gemma and I were just going to have some tea. It'll make you feel better. Come now and sit down."

"I have it just about all made," Gemma told her.

She didn't know what to say. Their kindness touched her and she wanted to cry again.

Dolly put everything on the table, and they all sat, sipping their tea in silence. Ciara couldn't think of a thing to have a pleasant conversation about.

"I feel so bad," Dolly suddenly stated. "I thought for sure there was something between you and Brogan." She glanced at Gemma, who was nodding.

The cup shook as Ciara set it down. The pain was so raw, but she needed to talk to someone. "I thought so too. He told me he loves me and that was the last I've seen of him. I think he regretted his words and is avoiding me. I know I'm no prize, and I've been nothing but a bother to him. I told him I couldn't be parted from Orla, and he agreed." She blinked back a tear. "I wish I never crossed that river into Texas. So much has happened in the last months, and I feel off center and hurt."

Gemma patted her hand for a moment. "I know when he looks at you his eyes shine with love. I hope he'll be back and soon."

Ciara nodded, not really agreeing. "He doesn't trust that anyone can love him. He said he'd made peace with it, but maybe he's still afraid of being hurt? I will not chase after him, and I don't want any of you asking him about it. It must be his decision. I just hope my heart can accept he's gone." She bit her bottom lip, wishing she knew what to do next.

"God is always with you," Dolly gently reminded her.

"Yes," Ciara agreed with a forced smile. It was so hard. When her parents died, everyone said it was God's will and she accepted it. It was getting harder and harder to accept things that happened. She stood. "Would you mind if I sat outside and cleared my head?"

"Of course not. Take your wrap, it's chilly." Dolly sent her an encouraging smile.

She took her thin wrap with her on her way out. Dolly was right, there was a chill in the air. She walked into the sunshine and felt warmed. She'd need to make some money to buy heavy wraps for her and Orla. Hadn't their mother expected the cold? She had left many things they needed behind. But she couldn't blame her parents for making the trip. Their farm had dried up, and nothing seemed to grow. Going West had sounded like a fine idea.

Life was ever changing, and she'd tried to bend and sway, going with the flow, but if she had to bend any further, she'd break. And she couldn't let that happen. Orla needed her to be strong. Oh, why had Brogan left her alone? She'd probably never know.

A horse raced toward her, and upon it coming closer, she recognized Sullivan. He jumped down before the horse stopped. "Where is everyone?"

It baffled her how they knew what to do, but his brothers all appeared. Sullivan's eyes held worry.

"I went to talk to Brogan, and there was a note on the table. Someone stole his horses, and he went after them. He wanted us to be sure to take care of the mares. I tossed them some hay and filled their water. But who knows when he left?" Sullivan looked into the eyes of each of his brothers. "I'm not sure where to start."

"The fence," Ciara said with sudden conviction. "The one that kept being taken down. It's at the end of his property about fifty yards from your place."

Sullivan gave a swift nod. "That's good information. Donnell, Murphy, Fitzpatrick, and Angus get your supplies. Bring extra ammunition. We'll meet back here in ten minutes. Teagan, Quinn, Rafferty, and Shea you must run both ranches."

"A sound plan," Teagan agreed. "Let's get their mounts saddled."

Ciara wrapped her arms around her quaking middle. "Do you think Brogan is all right?"

Quinn put his arm over her shoulder. "Sullivan would have told us if there'd been blood or any signs of a struggle. We need to have faith. A couple prayers would be nice. And have Orla go to Brogan's. I bet those mares need to be calmed and the cows milked."

"I will," she agreed, unable to keep the quaver out of her voice.

Quinn ran for the barn. As she stood there, it felt as

though a shard of ice was piercing her body. Supplies needed to be gathered. And that was something she could do. She ran into the house.

Brogan looked over his herd. Those lame-brained horse thieves had them in the nearest canyon. The three of them looked like young boys. There was no way he was hanging them. He just needed to scare them to near death. They'd taken off when they had first sighted him, but he didn't follow at first; he needed to check his horses.

Now he was on their trail and finding it easy to follow. He wouldn't be surprised if the horses didn't just make their way back to the ranch where the hay and grain were.

It wasn't much past noon, but the three boys had made a fire, and it looked as though they'd made camp for the night. Didn't they know to ride until they couldn't see? Quietly, he slid from his saddle, took his rifle, and saddlebag. He dropped the reins. Prince knew to stay put. He scouted the area more. There wasn't even much cover. Why'd they camp there?

There were no guns, that he could see. Slowly he walked toward them, an amiable smile pasted on his lips. "Howdy, boys."

The boys all stood and started to run, but they didn't go in the same direction, and they plowed each other to the ground.

"Haven't I seen you before?" Brogan asked, scrutinizing them. "Aren't you the Dixon boys?"

"We're men, not boys," the tallest one said. It didn't look as though the boy was old enough to shave yet.

"We hang men who steal horses," he casually said.

The other two boys gave the tall one mutinous looks. The

smallest one took a step forward. "Mister Brogan sir, I'm still a boy so you won't need to hang all three of us, just the other two."

The middle boy pushed the young one to the ground.

"Listen up," snapped Brogan. "Where is your pa?"

The tallest hung his head. "He got kilt in the war."

"Your ma?"

"We tried trapping and hunting, but we don't know much about either. Ma is sick and starving. You had all those horses all in one place and we thought… I don't know what we thought. Once we had them, we didn't know rightly what to do with 'em."

They were scared enough.

"What's your names?"

"I'm John, he's Fred, and the turncoat is Lars."

Lars stuck his tongue out at his older brother.

"I will take you with me. Where exactly do you live?"

"Not far," Fred said. "Do you know the place where the land is mostly rocks? That's where our cabin is."

"I see." How had these kids kept themselves alive for so long? Nothing grew in that area.

"I'm taking you home with me. Then I'll send some help to your Ma. I'll get you all fed, but you have to do something for me."

John kicked a rock. "Of course, you need somethin'."

What had these boys been through? Brogan shook his head. "I will show you how to trap and hunt and anything else a boy needs to know to be a man. Your part is to learn what I teach you. Understood?"

All three brown-headed boys nodded, and smiles broke across each face.

"Mount up. I'm taking you home with me."

ORLA STOOD at the downed fence greeting each horse as it stopped in front of her. "Are you sure you're counting them?" she asked Ciara.

"Yes, I'll get it right this time." When had Orla become so bossy?

"Brogan is fine, and he's riding this way."

Ciara shaded her eyes from the sun with her hand and peered about. "Where?"

"You'll see him soon. Melly here said she can feel the vibrations."

Ciara smiled. "You're usually right about these things."

"There he is!" Orla pointed in front of her.

The man she loved was riding out front, followed by three others. Was there trouble? Ciara grabbed her rifle off the ground. By this time, Teagan and Quinn both had run to be by her side. They made Orla stand behind them, but she didn't care as long as the horses could get to her.

As Brogan rode closer, they saw that he had three boys with him. Ciara dropped her firearm and ran toward Brogan and Prince. The next thing she knew, she was in his arms.

"I've missed you. I wanted nothing more than to tell you I had to trail after my horses, but I didn't think I'd have the time." He walked with her arm in arm to Teagan. "The boys' mother is real sick. Can one of you go for a doctor?" He explained where the cabin was, and Quinn took off toward town.

Rafferty took charge of the boys and brought them into the house to eat. He had them laughing by the time they went inside.

"Shall we?" Brogan asked Ciara and Orla.

"No, we only have thirty-two. There should be thirty-three horses," Orla insisted. "You go. I'll wait here."

"We'll wait with you. Which one is missing?" Brogan asked.

"Stewart. Melly said he'd have been here with the others, but some men caught him. She was sure at least one she already knew." Orla smiled.

"You named them all?" Brogan's eyes widened.

"Of course. Look! There they are!" Orla jumped up and down.

Sullivan, Donnell, Murphy, Fitzpatrick, and Angus rode through the break in the fence with the horse trailing behind.

"We made a good start," Angus said. "Brogan… you're here?"

"I told you the horses went back to the ranch," Sullivan muttered.

"Did you catch the outlaws too?" Murphy asked, looking confused.

"Yes, and thank you for bringing Stewart back."

Orla gave them an I-told-you-so smile. They all went into the house, and Brogan told them the story.

Sullivan stood. "I will go get Sheila Kelly. I doubt Doc is in town. I'll bring her to the Dixon Home."

As soon as he was gone, Fitzpatrick nodded. "I told you he was sweet on the little doctor gal."

"Sheila Kelly, now she'd make a good wife if anyone was looking, which none of us are. Well, maybe Brogan," Angus said while his face turned crimson.

"Ciara, can I talk to you outside, alone?" Brogan asked softly.

She nodded and led the way. Her stomach fluttered and then it churned.

He turned them so they were facing each other. "Ciara, I love you with every bit of love I have to give. Somehow you've become part of me, and I'm hoping you're thinking the same thing."

"What are you thinking of?" He was going to propose, she knew it.

"I'm going to need help with the boys until their ma is better."

Her heart dropped. "I see. You want me to come over every day and watch the boys?"

His brow furrowed and he stared at her. "You'd live here."

"Orla and I would share a room?" She thought she'd be sick.

"Where'd you get that idea? My wife sleeps with me. Orla will just have to get used to it."

"Your wife?" She studied the ground and held her breath, fearful of even hoping.

"Did I not ask you? I'm an idiot. Ciara, will you marry me?"

"Say yes!" the crowd inside shouted.

Ciara nodded. "I'd love nothing more."

"Yippee! I get to see the horses every day!" Orla yelled.

Ciara and Brogan shared a smile before he kissed her. It was so sweet, so tender, it made her feel so alive. He pulled back.

"What are you thinking about?"

"Faith."

EPILOGUE

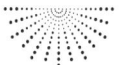

Ciara could hardly contain the joy within her. She was now a married woman. Her love knew no bounds. Brogan reached out and took her hand in his.

"The first dance is ours."

Ciara handed her bouquet to Orla and then she was pulled against her husband as the band played. They danced making use of the whole floor and she stared into his eyes.

"What are you thinking about?" he asked as he grinned.

"I was thanking God for you and Orla and my new family. I was thanking him that you patiently taught the Dixon boys how to hunt and then cut them in on your horse business. You're wonderful with children."

"They are fine boys and I'm just glad their ma is better."

"You want children, don't you?" She held her breath.

"I want to have children with you; as many as God blesses us with. We may have to enlarge the house someday."

Her face heated and she knew it was the reddest of red. "I'm nervous about tonight."

"So am I," he whispered into her ear.

She pulled back and saw the truth in his eyes. "It can't be too hard. All married people do it. Just be gentle."

"I'll always be gentle with you, my love. I will treasure you for the rest of my life as I give thanks."

She felt a tap on her shoulder and frowned as she turned.

"May I cut in?" Orla asked.

"Yes." Ciara pulled back from Brogan and waited for her to take his outstretched hand. Instead Orla took Ciara's hand and tried to dance with her.

Ciara laughed. "Orla what are you doing?"

"I never get a moment alone with you. I wanted you to know Dolly invited me for a sleepover. That's what she called it, so I imagine I'm spending the night. Gemma and Teagan will be there, so you won't have to worry. Brogan will be with you in case you get scared. It's been a long time since we've slept apart." Orla sounded excited, serious, and then sad.

"But you'll be back, and you'll stay with Brogan and me. And the horses."

"Tell Brogan not to worry the mares won't be birthing tonight. The next couple weeks will be busy." Orla took her hand and dragged her to Brogan. "Don't forget to tell him."

Brogan kissed Ciara and she tingled from head to toe. "Tell me what?"

"Orla said the mares will not be birthing tonight but the next couple of weeks will be busy."

He nodded. "Good to know. They were on my mind. I hoped that we'd have some privacy tonight without having to help to foal. Have I told you today I love you?"

She smiled. "Once an hour at least. I love you too."

"That's why I keep saying it, I like to hear you say it back." He hugged her to him. "You are the greatest risk I've ever taken and I'm so glad you thawed my frozen heart."

"I'll keep it warm always."

They stood arm in arm watching the others dance. It was one of the best days in her life and she often told the story of how she and Brogan met. All their daughters found it to be so romantic.

THE END

Thank you for spending time with the Kavanagh brothers. Brogan was a hard nut to crack, but he eventually gave his heart. Next up is Sullivan's Story. Do you remember the healer Sheila Kelly? They are the two most independent, stubborn people in a time where women were not encouraged to be independent or in some cases have opinions. Will Sullivan learn that the way to a woman's heart is not telling her what to do with her life? Join me for some life-threatening adventure and grand romance!

Kathleen Ball

SULLIVAN: COWBOY PROTECTOR

Shelia Kelly leaned over bracing her hand against the rough tree trunk. Her lungs burned and her legs felt like rubber. She breathed so hard it was hard to hear if she was still being pursued. She'd dealt with all kinds, but she'd never been chased by men with rifles.

The word witch could be heard and she took off running again. There wasn't a way to save the little girl, she'd lost too much blood. She'd died as soon as they brought her into her cabin. They put the blame on her and when they mentioned burning her at the stake, she took off running out the back door.

Her face, hands and arms were covered in scratched from the limbs of the trees and bushes. A few were deep but that didn't matter. Where was she supposed to go? Those men would get the whole town roused against her and they'd hang her. She had to get Becca her daughter.

"Ugh." She hit the ground hard as she tripped on a root. Her nose was bleeding, and her ankle throbbed. Still she needed to get away. Think, think, what to do. Would they expect her to run to town to get help? She turned north until she came to a fence.

Going any further was impossible. She slumped against a tree near the fence and lay on the ground, hoping the underbrush would hide her.

Closing her eyes, she prayed for protection. She was a healer not a witch. She'd healed so many of the people who lived in the area, but today all good deeds went out the window and blew away to be forgotten. She was mostly forgotten unless someone couldn't get to the doctor or the doctor was away. Otherwise she lived a hermit type of life and had since she was thirteen.

Breathing became easier and her nose stopped bleeding. When it was safe she'd make herself a crutch from branches and go where no one could find her. Waiting until dark would be for the best. Now if only she could get her heart to stop pounding.

The pounding of hooves alerted her. They sounded to be coming from all sides. This was it.

One horse and rider were on the other side of the fence while the other was almost steeping on her. The quaking of her body wouldn't stop.

"Howdy Russ," a familiar voice greeted.

"Kavanagh, I'm looking for that healing woman. She killed little Jenny Wren. I need to talk to her."

"Saw her last week. She was home with her daughter."

"Thanks Kavanagh, I'll keep looking," Russ said sounding determined.

As soon as he rode away, she opened her eyes and saw Sullivan vault the fence. "It's just me," he said in a low voice.

"I need your help, Sullivan. Becca is at Widow Muse's place and I need to get her before they take her away." Tears escaped her eyes and trailed down her face.

Sullivan kneeled before her. His blue eyes were full of

determination. His eyes and his strong jaw made her feel a bit better.

"I can't walk, I hurt my ankle. I could walk with a crutch. I'd rather just stay here if you'd get Becca for me."

"I'd feel better getting you home first."

"No get Becca please?"

He reached forward and wiped a tear off her face. He stood and looked around and handed Sheila a branch that could serve as a crutch. "Donnell and Murphy are supposed to be checking the grass to make sure there aren't any poisonous plants for the cattle to get into. Wave them down if you see them and have them bring you to the house."

"Thank you, Sullivan,—" He'd already jumped the fence, got on his bay and was riding away.

***

Didn't people understand Sheila didn't have a mean bone in her body? He hoped he didn't meet any armed yahoos out in the forest. Russ' friends were the shoot first ask questions later type. He rode slowly and silently. He made it to the widow's house without a problem. He tied Zealous at the back of the widow's house.

The back door opened. "Take her to safety. They were already here, and I bet they'll be back. Bless you Sullivan." She handed him the dark-haired girl in her arms.

"You be careful," he told the widow. He mounted the horse with Becca in his arms and slowly rode away.

Becca kept turning trying to see his face and he leaned down to her ear. "We need to be so very quiet. I'm taking you to your ma."

Her head dropped forward and he hugged her to him for a moment. She was such a quiet child to begin with. There were kids on the Kavanagh ranch she could play with.

Sullivan was confident his nine brothers would help him to keep Sheila and Becca safe. His gut tightened thinking about Sheila and Becca being in danger. He urged Zealous to go faster. It didn't take long before he was at the ranch house. He swung down with Becca in his arms.

"You'd best get her inside," Donnell advised. "Sheila is all kinds of worried."

He nodded his thanks and he practically raced up the steps of the big ranch house. Once in the door, Becca squirmed until she was standing on the floor. She flew into her mother's arms and began to cry.

"Are you hurt? Let me look at you." Sheila peeled Becca's arms from around her neck. "Did anyone touch you?"

Becca shook her head. "Just Sullivan. I like him but I was scared." She dove into Sheila's arms again.

Sheila met his gaze and mouthed "thank you". The fear in her eyes got to him. Sheila was as fearless as they came. It wasn't easy raising a child alone. Sheila made it look easy.

His relief of Sheila's safety engulfed him and it made him uneasy. He liked to care but this was bordering on caring too much.

Dolly bustled out of the kitchen. She set a cup of tea and a glass of milk on the table. She peered at Sullivan and he nodded his gratitude. Dolly had been taking care of the family for as long as he could remember. With their parents gone she took on the role of mother and friend. She went back into the kitchen returning with a plate of cookies and her own cup of tea.

"It sounds like you both had an awful fright." She put the cookies on the table in front of mother and daughter and then she sat on one of the chairs near the sofa. "Did you manage to bring any of your things with you?"

"It all happened to fast. It was all I could do to escape. Jenny Wren's father carried her into the house. She was already dead, but he didn't want to believe me. The next thing I know he started yelling it was my fault the girl had died. Russ and a few of his friends were outside and that's when I heard them talking about burning the witch. I saw them head for my front door and I ran out the back and down a hidden path."

"You poor dear." Dolly commiserated.

Teagan the oldest of the brothers ran into the house and Gemma his wife hurried down the stairs. Gemma shouldn't have gone down the steps so quick, she was heavy with child and out of breath. Teagan seated her.

"Oh your ankle is black and blue!" Gemma exclaimed.

Dolly immediately stood. "I'll get a cold wet cloth to wrap it. Donnell pull the table closer so I can put her leg up on it."

Sullivan helped Donnell. Dolly came back with the cloth and wrapped Sheila's ankle.

"That feels better. Thank you."

"What else do you need? You probably know a plant to cure it."

"Actually Sullivan if you have any of that liniment I gave you for the horses that would be wonderful." She glanced at Dolly and then at Gemma. "I have cuts that need stitches. Are either of you—?"

"Your best bet is to have Sullivan do it. He has a way of doing it that makes a scar less noticeable." Gemma nodded in agreement.

"Sullivan carry her to the front bedroom. It has a big bed Sheila and Becca can share," Dolly instructed.

"I'll get the water heated and gather the soap, cloths, thread and needle," Gemma volunteered as she struggled to get up from the plush chair. She laughed and held out her hands for Teagan to take.

"Gemma, I'll do all that," Dolly instructed. "Donnell could you go over to Quinn's place and see if Heaven can bring the kids over to keep Becca company?" She turned and stared at

Sullivan. "Well? What are you waiting for?" "Oh Donnell grab the liniment while you're out."

Teagan and Gemma exchanged amused glances.

"Teagan you hurry on ahead of Sullivan and make sure the bed covers are turned down."

Sullivan's lips twitched. Dolly was good in a crisis, but he never noticed how bossy she actually was.

"Ready?" He gazed into Sheila's dark eyes. When she nodded he lifted her into his arms. "You can help too Becca."

Sheila wrapped her arms around his neck and he could feel her warm breath on his neck. It warmed his whole insides. He made his strides a bit longer; he needed to put her down. He was not in the market for a female especially a carefree one who thumbs her nose at all rules. She was very attractive, and he enjoyed talking with her but that was where it stopped.

Teagan turned down the bed and Sullivan gently put Sheila on it.

Why was he the one who was to stich her up? Gemma, Ciara or Heaven all probably sewed. It was going to be very awkward touching her skin. Hopefully it was just her arm or something.

Soon enough everything was brought into the room and everyone was ushered out except for him. This couldn't be proper at all but Shelia didn't seem bothered by it.

"I could ask one of the women to stay in here."

"We're adults, Sullivan. Open the door if you're concerned."

He did just that but he still didn't feel right.

Chapter Two

They'd become good friends and now Sullivan acted as though she was contagious. Had she done or said something wrong? His was the one friendship she treasured. He never wanted anything from her. He was different from a lot of the men in town. They assumed her to be a lonely widow.

"I'll need to take my dress off but I have proper undergarments and of course we'll use the sheet to cover me." Usually she said it to the patients to make them comfortable. She unbuttoned her dress and slid it off. "Worse than I thought. I can do it myself, Sullivan."

He turned and saw her shoulders and back. "What happened?"

"Running through the woods and falling." She fisted her hands.

"Painful?"

"Yes, and I don't have my willow bark tea. It's fine just get started. Clean the wound before you stitch."

"I have some whiskey. I bet it would help with the pain."

Her eyes widened and she shuddered. "No thank you." She shivered. "I don't drink whiskey."

He carefully cleaned two spots on her left side. "I'm going to have to sit on the bed to reach the first one."

"That's fine." She gritted her teeth as the needle went in. Deep breathing helped to manage the pain a bit.

Teagan surprised her by entering the room. "Gemma sent this up for you to drink." He handed her the teacup.

She smelled it and smiled. "Willow bark. Tell Gemma I thank her." She drank it and waited for it's effect. Her body began to relax slightly.

"Do you need me, Sullivan?"

"I'm almost done. Make sure you leave the door open," he quipped.

Teagan chuckled. "I'm not worried. You are always the protector not the one who causes trouble."

Sheila turned to give Sullivan easier access to the other side of her back. She tried not to flinch at even his softest of touches but she'd never been able to help it. Despite the willow bark tea her mind kept repeating what happened that day. People didn't believe in witches anymore did they? Mr. Wren certainly got people believing enough to search for her.

She needed her rainy-day money and she needed to take her daughter and run. She'd been wise enough to have bags packed and money hidden but she didn't plan where to go. Texas was a big state but much of It was unsettled. They weren't awfully far from Oklahoma. She could find a job that didn't involve her vast knowledge of healing.

"What do you know about Oklahoma?" she asked trying to keep her voice nice and light.

"Not all that much. It's not a territory yet and there are plenty of Indians, Choctaw Indians. It's settled some but you can't expect any help if the Indians decide they want you off their land."

"That bad, huh? My family has lived in this area for generations. They must have had to fight to keep their land at some point. I think I'm the first to be run off." Frustration had a hold on her.

"You planning on taking a trip?" She couldn't see his face but she could tell from his voice he didn't approve. She'd never needed any man's approval and never intended to.

"I need to take Becca to a safe place. I'm not sure which way I plan to go. I also need to stop by my place and grab a few things and then dig up my money."

"You might want to wait a few days. Your house is certain to be watched."

Pounding on the front door caused her to jump. "I'll just go with them, unless there's another way out of here. Most don't know I have a child."

"Stay put." he stared at her. "I mean it."

She gave him a curt nod. But he'd soon learn he couldn't boss her around.

***

Sullivan joined the rest downstairs and nodded to the man Russ from that morning. "What's going on?" Sullivan asked Teagan.

"Russ here says Sheila Kelly killed a girl but he doesn't know how she did it. Something smells fishy about the whole story."

Sullivan turned to Russ. "How was she killed? Did Sheila shoot her?"

"No, nothing like that. Ed brought his daughter into the Kelly place and the next thing we knew, Jenny was dead."

"But how sick was she and why did ed bring her there?" Sullivan gazed intently at Russ.

"The way I heard it, Jenny caught her dress on fire while watching her ma wash clothes. They soaked her in water for a longtime then one of the men was called to go get the doc but he wasn't there. I guess they dressed Jenny and brought her to the witches house." Russ shrugged.

"Have you ever seen a burned person, Russ?" Teagan asked. "Cold water helps a bit but it's hard to see. She would have been in too much pain for them to put clothes on her. Unless maybe they drugged her. Give too much and it can kill a person."

"She was limp and dressed with her eyes closed. That's all I know. You make some good points but I doubt you'd be able to change Mr. Wren's mind. He told me once that Shelia had put a curse on him and he believed it. I'll go back but I know my voice wont be heard above the rest of the men out for blood."

Becca walked to Sullivan and held her arms up to him. He immediately picked her up and snuggled her close.

Russ stared at him. "I never knew you had a child."

Sullivan smiled. "She's my pride and joy." He wasn't about to mention her name.

Teagan walked Russ to the door and practically pushed him out.

"He won't be the last to come here," Gemma said. "That poor girl must have been dead before they dressed her."

"I'll carry Becca upstairs. Dolly could you please make up a tray for them? I think we'll need to move them tomorrow."

The door opened again. Surprise crossed his brother Brogan's face. "You do have them and they're safe. I just got a visit. I have a feeling they won't stop until they find Sheila.

"Good to see you Brogan," Dolly said as she started to climb the steps with a platter of food. Sullivan walked behind her carrying the little girl.

"Teagan we'd better list possibilities of hideouts," Brogan said.

Sullivan smiled at Becca. He should have protected them somehow. He should have seen this coming. There must have been something he could have done. As soon as they walked into the room, Becca squirmed down and ran to her mother.

The affection between the two always marveled Sullivan. It was a sight to behold. Shelia winced and Sullivan lifted Becca and sat her on the bed right next to her mother.

"There, this way you can both eat supper in bed."

Shelia mouthed thank you to him.

"If you need anything just holler," Dolly told her as she bustled out the room.

Sullivan put the tray on Shelia's lap and sat on the bed, helping Becca. She was a good eater and polite too.

"We'll have to move you tomorrow," he casually told Sheila.

Her eyes filled with fear. "What do you mean? I thought it would just blow over."

"I don't think it will go that way for now. Don't worry, I'll be with you every step of the way."

"I still need to get my clothes, medicines and my money."

Her voice grew louder.

"It'll have to wait."

"Take the tray off me. Take it now!"

He lifted and she scrambled out of bed. She turned toward him. "I don't like people telling what to do. I have my own life." She paced in front of the bed. "I want to be consulted on decisions. I'm not a mindless person who just follows the dictate of others. If you don't mind I can help my daughter."

She waited until he left the room and then she shut the door.

He went downstairs and Donnell's eyes were full of humor. "Kicked you out didn't she?"

Sullivan rubbed the back of his neck.

"We all know you're sweet on her," Donnell teased.

It would have been so easy to just punch Donnell and get his frustrations out that way. "It doesn't matter. We need to see to her safety." He brushed by Donnell hitting his should with his own shoulder.

"She wants to be consulted in any decisions. I'm not sure that's in her best interest."

Gemma and Dolly both turned on him at the same time giving him shocked expressions.

"Sullivan Kavanagh, sit!" Dolly pointed to one of the wooden chairs at the table.

First and last name, he must have done something wrong. He sat and waited.

"Does she have a condition I don't know about? Are her thoughts scrambled?" She ut her hands on her hips as she stared at him.

"No, ma'am." His brothers snickered in the background.

"She's been raising that beautiful girl all by herself for some time now hasn't she?"

He slowly nodded.

"Then what makes you think you can run her life without asking her? You might think of her as a damsel in distress but she's not incapable of taking care of herself. Do you think Gemma, Ciara or Heaven would allow their husbands to tell them what to do?"

Sullivan pushed back his chair causing a loud scrapping noise. "I get the point. I'm not stupid."

Dolly hurried over and hugged Sullivan. "No one said you were. It's just that I see how you two looked at each other when the other isn't looking. Don't push her away."

He took a deep breath and gritted his teeth. They didn't understand him at all. "Let's get a few ideas so we can ask her what she'd like to do."

The door opened again and this time his brothers all filed in, Donnell, Murphy, Fitzpatrick, Angus, Rafferty and finally Shea.

"Horses coming. A lot of them," one of his brothers announced.

Quinn came in the back with Heaven, Owen, Tim, Daisy with Ciara and Orla. Orla locked the door behind her.

Brogan put his arm around Ciara and nodded at his sister-in-law Orla.

"Women and children upstairs and stay down away from the windows," Teagan yelled right before he kissed Gemma.

The brothers all scrambled for extra ammo. Then Quinn put out the lanterns while everyone took their places near the windows.

"Why are they back?" Donnell asked.

"They must know Sheila and Becca are here," Murphy answered.

"Russ saw Becca and someone probably told him I don't have a daughter," Sullivan said sounding frustrated.

Continue Reading

TEAGAN: COWBOY STRONG

Teagan Kavanagh pushed his hat back and frowned as he stared out over his pasture, dotted with grazing livestock. He shook his head and looked again. A good many of the cattle on his land didn't belong to him. "Tarnation!" he muttered as the truth dawned on him. Someone had knocked down the fence again.

Running his gaze over the fence in the distance, it didn't take him long to spot the breach. It was hard not to see considering several scrawny cows were jumping over the downed posts and wire and roaming onto his land as he watched. Still mumbling under his breath, he spurred his dun, Sandy through the hole in the fence and rode for the Maguire house.

The broken steps, unpatched roof, and the door barely hanging on its hinges surprised him. Why was the place in such disrepair? It couldn't cost that much to fix it up. They had plenty of cattle. Maybe they didn't know that because they were all on his land grazing on his grass.

The squawking of the chickens was the only sign that

anything alive was around. The ground was nothing but patches of dirt that blew like dust in the scorching Texas sun.

Teagan swung down off his horse, by-passed the porch steps and knocked on the house instead of the door. He waited, but nothing happened. No one answered. He hopped off the porch and went around back. The garden that had once been lush and vibrant with vegetables was no longer anything but a patch of weeds. But laundry on the clothesline was whipping in the wind. Someone lived here.

Then he saw her, Gemma Maguire. She was pulling with what seemed to be all her might on a rope around their old cow. It always was a stubborn animal, and time hadn't mellowed her one bit. He strode over and, without so much as a word of greeting, took the rope out of Gemma's hand, and with a firm tug to get her moving, he led Old Bennie into the falling-down barn and to her stall. He removed the rope and closed the stall door behind him when he was done.

When he turned around and walked out of the barn, she was waiting for him just outside the door.

"Gemma," he said in a neutral tone as he tipped his hat to her.

"Teagan. I heard all the boys made it home from the war. What a blessing." She quickly stared at the ground and shuffled her feet a bit. "I guess you want to evict me. I'm trying to locate any family I might have, plus the bank said I still had one month before I had to either pay off the loan or leave." Her chin wavered, and she swallowed hard. "I… suppose you could say I've hit on hard times."

"Where are your folks?"

"Mama died of consumption, and Daddy never did come back from the war. I married a man who promised to take care of the ranch and me, but he took all my money and left. I guess I wasn't very good at picking a husband. He tried to sell the land right from under me but there was too much debt, all his debt. He liked to play cards at Bobbie's Saloon for days at a time." She stole a quick look at him and bowed her head again. "I will pack."

"I didn't buy your ranch, Gemma."

She narrowed her eyes as she stared at him. "Of course, you did. Mr. Lyons told me how you wanted me gone right away but he worked it out so I could stay until the end of the month. He said Teagan Kavanagh bought the place with cash."

He shook his head, trying to make sense of her words. "I don't understand any of this. When's the last time you had a good meal?"

She turned crimson. "It's not important."

He touched her arm and was struck by a jolt of awareness; he still felt a spark between them after all this time. "It is important. I hate to say this Gemma, but you look worse than the beggars in the city."

Stepping away, she turned her back on him. "I will be out by the end of the month." Gemma lifted her skirt a bit and ran to the house. She almost fell on the busted-up steps, and she was extremely gentle with the door.

They had once been such good friends. Good friends until he'd asked her to marry him, at least… and she said no. He hadn't even been aware she got married. He supposed he had never really known her at all. His hands fisted as he walked to Sandy then swung up into the saddle.

A wry chuckle bubbled forth. He never had gotten to the reason he'd come over; the cattle.

As he rode, he couldn't help but compare the worn-down woman he'd just left to the vital young lady she'd once been. Her blossom of youth had vanished, her hair looked uncombed, and her dress has seen better days. *"I married a man who promised to take care of the ranch and me…"* Her words echoed in his head, and he couldn't get the broken look she'd worn as she told him out of his mind. *She married someone else.* The notion was pure torture and would not leave him alone while he rode through his herd and got a better sense of how many head she had on his property.

Heading home and asking his brothers a few questions might clear things up. Then he would see Victor Lyons and find out why Gemma thought he was buying her ranch.

She hadn't set eyes on him for at least six years. He'd grown up, hardened some, but mostly he was the same. She'd fallen for him the minute she first saw him with his broad shoulders, sky-blue eyes, and brown hair. He'd been confident bordering on arrogance back then. He seemed more reserved now. She'd spent far too much time crying over that man.

Her father had hated the whole Kavanagh family, and he'd forbidden her to marry Teagan. In fact, the day Teagan had asked her, she had been ordered to tell him he'd be shot on sight if he came near her again. The confusion and hurt in his eyes had haunted her all these years. When the Kavanagh boys joined up to fight the war, she'd been terrified he'd be killed.

At first, she had ridden the fence line between their ranches to glean a bit of information about how he was doing, but none of the brothers would talk to her. Losing their friendship had cut deep, but she didn't have a choice. Her father never told her why he hated Mr. Kavanagh.

She prayed so much for the boys in gray. Then her father had joined the army and soon after that, her mother had died. What a terrible time it was. Few folks helped her, and she had never understood why. Her mother had been friendly to them all.

Then the soldiers had raided her food. She dug a new

root cellar, but it was discovered, and the army took her food. Finally, she walked a good half hour and dug another new one. She planted her garden out there too, after the one near her house had been raided to the extent there was nothing left. She'd been lucky she'd had enough time to grow and harvest again.

She'd picked all the wild berries she could find and made preserves. It was a long trek in the winter, and she spent much of the time covering her tracks. It was a lonely time, and though they were her nearest neighbors, not one of the Kavanaghs had checked on her. She paid the mortgage every month with money she'd found buried in her yard. Her father hadn't trusted banks. As far as she'd known everything had been paid off.

It had proven a struggle, but she had been getting by. One day after church, a handsome man with blond hair and brown eyes had smiled at her. He'd asked her to go for a walk. He was funny and charming. His manners were polished, and he was so respectful. The other unmarried women in the town all had their eyes on him, but every Sunday he'd chosen her. She'd been too smitten by his attentions to realize she was just being played for a fool.

Shoving the memories aside, she stared out the window and into her ruined garden. If Teagan didn't know about the land buy, then what was going on? It was time—past time,— for answers. She'd need to draw a hot bath and press her Sunday dress, for tomorrow she was going to the Kavanagh's.

It was a bit of a walk to the Kavanagh's house; a dry, hot, sweaty walk. Hopefully her shoes would hold together. She could see the house and outbuildings from a distance, and the difference between the state of their house and hers shamed her. The Kavanagh house was beautifully whitewashed, and she had always admired the big porch. A person could walk out any door of the house and be on the porch. Their steps looked to be in fine condition, and she'd bet they didn't have water leaking into the house when it rained. To think her house had once been in such fine order as that.

A sigh slipped past her lips, and she squared her shoulders. She'd done the best she could, and she'd survived. She had made some bad, life-altering decisions, but here she was. Which of the boys would answer the door? Or did they still have Dolly working for them? She had checked the notices of death constantly and she had never seen the name Kavanagh on any of them, but the notices weren't always correct.

She stood very straight and tall and hesitated. Teagan wouldn't want to see her. She'd lost her pride when she told him about her life. What had she been thinking? A hush seemed to settle around her. No birdsong, no chirp and hum of insects. No voices. No one was around. She should turn around and leave…

The door swung inward, and the Kavanagh's housekeeper stood framed in the opening. "Mrs. Parks," Dolly greeted. "I saw you walk up, but I didn't hear you knock. Well, come on in. I haven't seen you in a while not since… Well, it's been a while."

Gemma walked in. "It's good to see you too, Dolly." Gemma had always admired the woman who had practically raised the boys. Dolly had black hair she wore braided. It hung down her back and was as thick as a man's wrist. She was older and she ruled the house with an iron hand. It was as though she was the conscience of the household. The boys had often looked to her for advice.

"I was just making some tea. Would you care to join me?" Dolly tilted her head slightly, and her smile was welcoming, but not as warm as normal, as though she knew this wasn't a social call.

"That sounds lovely. Is Teagan available? I need to talk to him."

Dolly shook her head. "He grumbled about bankers and went to town."

Gemma's heart quickened. So, he knew about the sale. She gave a nod. "The tea sounds good if you're still offering."

"Of course. Please have a seat, and I'll be right back."

Dolly walked to the kitchen, and with each step she took, Gemma lost a bit more of her confidence. Dolly had such poise and manners. Gemma felt like a country hick compared to her. She sat in a comfortable chair facing the lavish stone fireplace that took up half the wall. It was beautiful when lit during a frigid day. At least that was how she remembered it.

Was Teagan chastising the banker for telling her who had bought the land? Did she have any prayer of paying him off? Would he help her? She must have a few stray cattle somewhere, but without a horse to round them up, she couldn't claim them as collateral against any debt. No, she'd drink her tea as quickly as she could while still being polite and then she was leaving. Coming here was just another bad decision to add to her long list.

Dolly returned with a tray that held the tea and sugar cookies to have with it. Gemma's mouth watered as she stared at those cookies. Dolly poured a cup of tea and handed it over. "If I remember you like it plain?"

"Yes, thank you." Gemma waited for Dolly to be seated before she took a sip. It was heavenly. She hadn't had tea in a while, so she savored each sip. The sugar cookie had extra sugar sprinkled on top. It had been a long while since she'd had sugar.

"Oh, Teagan is back," Dolly announced as she hopped up and opened the door for him. "You have a visitor.

Teagan glanced at her and didn't bother to hide his scowl. "Miss. Maguire, please come with me to my office."

"Mrs. Parks," Dolly corrected.

Gemma stood. Her face heated. "It's still Maguire. My husband already had a wife when he married me." Shamed, she walked to the office, now Teagan's office. It still looked and smelled the same. Everything was made of leather and there was still a hint of the scent of his father's pipe tobacco in the air.

Teagan caught up and closed the door. "Please have a seat."

She remained standing. "Dolly told me you went to see Mr. Lyons?" she pressed. No sense stalling, she decided as she met his gaze.

Teagan took his time getting settled behind the massive wooden desk. "What we have is a bit of a mystery. Mr. Lyons didn't have any signed papers from a buyer. Interestingly enough, you are not behind on your payments, so I don't understand why he told you to leave at the end of the month. At first, he pretended to not know what I was talking about. He was lying. He's still lying, but now he can't hold anything over you. I took the liberty of paying off your debt, and the house and land are yours."

"You—*what?*" Why would he do something like that? And how…? She forced her racing mind to slow down so she could have a civil conversation with him. "I'll pay you back every cent." She would just have to figure out how. "I-I can't even pretend to know what is going on." She sank down on one of the leather chairs. "I had the land and everything all paid for. It took a lot of going without, but I didn't mind. I didn't want anyone to think they could take it after the war. But then… Well, my husband…" She wrung her hands. "I'll pay you the first of the month." She stood and turned toward the door.

"Wait! How do you expect to pay me?"

"Well... I must have some cattle... somewhere."

He gave a curt nod. "You do, currently grazing on my land. How do expect to round them up? You don't have a horse, do you?"

"Just how many cattle are we talking about? I figured I had a few hiding in a canyon or something."

He was going to tell her to get off the property. Saying that she had no business running a ranch.

"I'm sorry your first husband didn't work out," Teagan said gently. "But you need help. I'll figure out which of my brothers will marry you."

The breath left her lungs in a whoosh. "You will *what?* Listen *Mr.* Kavanagh, you may be able to tell people on this ranch what to do, but I'm not one of them." She gave him a hard, angry stare. Arrange for her to marry one of his brothers? How absurd!

"Where do you plan to go?"

"It's none of your business."

"Yes, it is. All right, I lied. I paid it off, and I hold the note on the property. The only way I'm getting paid back is if you have a husband to rebuild the ranch."

"You take too much upon yourself. I will never marry again."

"Is there one brother over another you'd prefer?" He sat back and crossed his arms.

Her heart jumped. The fight went out of her momentarily as she stared into his eyes. Yes, there was, but he'd never believe her. "I won't subject any of your brothers to a loveless marriage."

"Is that what you had, a loveless marriage?" His voice turned taunting.

"Yes, if you must know. I settled and I knew it, but I didn't know just how hard it could be. The man I really loved was always on my mind, and Richard was well aware who that was. He threw it in my face every chance he got. He spent more time at Bobbie's Saloon than he did at home, and he wasn't always gambling. People whispered about it every time I was in town." She heaved a sigh. "But that was my burden to bear. I refuse to marry again. I had my heart torn out once, and I won't do it again." She opened the door and walked out of the office.

Just who did he think he was? *"You don't have a horse, do you?"* he'd said, as if that would solve all her problems. Well, she had two good feet; she'd drag her cattle back. A soft snarl curled her lip as she thought about her cattle on Kavanagh land. That no-good banker had led her to believe they'd been rustled. She knew the Kavanaghs weren't thieves. She walked and walked, aware that her shoes were rubbing her feet raw, limping more with each painful step.

The door to the house was off its hinges and on the ground. Had someone been there? Did she dare check inside? She grabbed the axe off the chopping stump and walked to the door then cautiously pushed it open. No one was there. In fact, nothing was there; all her things had been taken, furniture and all. What was going on? She'd had to be strong for so long… And now she not only didn't have a horse, she had nothing. Great gasping sobs tore through her body.

She sat on the porch and cried.

Continue Reading

GREG

At the loud crack of a rifle shot and the subsequent bullet whizzing by his head, Greg Settler dove for the ground. He'd barely lifted his head when another shot rang out, kicking up the dirt next to him.

Jumping Jehoshaphat! What was going on? He'd finally arrived in California and drove his pickaxe into the ground to stake his claim. Not a minute later he was waiting for death. He'd heard the Goldmines of California were dangerous but he hadn't imagined anything like the situation he was in now. Afraid to move, he crouched behind a bush, his mind raced for a solution.

"I'll cover you! Make a run over here!" A voice to his right called out. "Ready? One, two, three, run!!"

Greg had never gotten up and sprinted faster in his life. He dove into the dark cave-like opening in the mountain, gulping for air. "Thank you."

A few more shots were exchanged before all was quiet. He glanced around the beginnings of a shaft mine. The front was shored up with lumber and it served as this man's living quarters too.

GREG

The man quickly put out the oil lamp and sat in the dark shadow keeping watch across the stream.

Greg sat up and leaned back against the side of the shaft. "What was that all about?"

The man turned toward Greg. Only he wasn't a man at all, and Greg's breath caught with his surprise. Although it was dark, he could make out her features. She was quite pretty with bow-shaped lips and long blond hair. He couldn't tell the color of her eyes. For some reason, that bothered him.

"It's simple really, someone wants your claim." Her voice flowed like honey, and he wondered how he'd ever mistaken her for a man.

"I haven't even started it."

"You drove your pickaxe into the soil. You started it all right. I'm just glad I was here to help. My pa went for supplies, and I'm guarding our claim. It wasn't necessary a month ago, but some color was found a couple claims down and now everyone thinks this place has gold on the ground ripe for picking. They'll turn this area into another boomtown and bring all its problems with it."

"I'm Greg Settler from Oregon." He put out his hand.

She wiped her palm on her pants before accepting his handshake. "I'm Mercy Watkins. You'll find out soon enough that you can never seem to be mud-free out here."

Greg smiled. "Been out here long?"

"If it's not one claim it's another. My pa has gold fever. We've been at it since March of 1849. We make enough to keep us fed."

He cocked his brow. "It would seem like a female—"

"Don't say it. I'm a hard worker, and there's nowhere else I'd rather be," she said in a defensive tone.

"I'm sorry. No insult intended. I have two sisters, Scarlett and Cindy. Both hard workers, but boy does Scarlett love her dresses. Cindy is more of a homebody, but... I'm not saying it right. My pa has a way with words, not me. It's admirable that you are a hard worker and helping your pa."

Her laugh was smooth like a fine Kentucky whiskey. "No harm done. I'm used to men telling me to go find a husband and a home to live in. To me this is my home."

She put down the heavy canvas flaps that covered the front of the mine and then lit the lamp. "I've got coffee and bread if you'd like some."

Greg swallowed hard. She had the greenest eyes he'd ever seen. She was beautiful in the lamplight. Her honeyed blond hair curled as it spilled down her back. She was also covered in dried mud. People told her to marry? She appeared too young to get married.

"Much obliged. I have some food and supplies on my claim, but I suppose it isn't safe to be on it at the moment."

"That's why you need to sit by the door with my rifle and keep watch over your things." She handed him the rife and the bullets. "My pa will whistle three times so don't shoot him by accident."

Greg loaded the rifle and took up post at the front of the claim. He was off to the side and had a good view between the flaps. "Does this mean I won't be sleeping ever?"

Mercy handed him a cup of coffee and she placed a tin plate of bread next to him. "It's best to have a partner. I guess you have gold fever too."

"It would be nice to earn my fortune, but I really just wanted to do something that was my own. I want to build something and make something of my life."

She glanced at him. "They threw you out of the house, did they?"

He furrowed his brow. "They most certainly did not. In fact tears were involved when I left."

"Hope you had a bandanna to mop up your face as you rode away." She laughed her whiskey laugh again.

"I come from a family made up of orphans from the Oregon Trail. Our ma and pa taught us to think for ourselves and make something of ourselves. We live on a big ranch, and I could have stayed but I wanted to try something different. Restless feet, I guess."

"A big family sounds really nice." He could hear the longing in her voice.

Three short whistles from outside interrupted them.

"Pa's home."

A large man with wide shoulders pushed through the flaps with a large crate in his hands. He dropped the crate and reached for his gun.

"Pa, don't. This is our new neighbor, Greg Settler. He was being shot at, so I took pity on him."

Her pa looked Greg up and down before he nodded and took his hand off the butt of his gun. "I'm Hugo. It's nice to meet you. You've never mined before, have ya?"

"Nice to meet you sir, and no I haven't."

"Just call me Hugo. We don't go by ceremony around here. Mercy probably told you someone struck gold nearby. Now we have all kinds wandering about. We can take turns keeping watch tonight, and tomorrow we'll get your tent up. You did bring a tent, didn't you?"

Greg turned his attention to guarding his mine. "I certainly did and probably a lot of useless stuff. They recommend everything at the supply store in Hang Town."

"Where's your horse or did you come by boat and then walk?" Hugo questioned.

Greg didn't take his eyes off his claim. "I traded my horse for a mule."

Mercy laughed so loud that Greg glanced her way and saw her shoulders shaking hard.

"What?"

"Your horse was probably worth ten times what Ole Blue is worth," Hugo said in amusement.

"Ole Blue? How'd you know the name of my mule?" Greg was getting tired of being laughed at.

"Ole Blue is traded to new miners. Usually to the ones the stable owner, Hank, thinks will quit fast. They always bring him back the mule and Hanks trades the same mule to the next new miner. Don't worry. Ole Blue is a good mule." Hugo rummaged through the crate. "I can add a can of beans to your bread if you like."

"That's mighty good of you." Greg had found that refusing this far West was the same as an insult. He shifted his attention back outside, glad to have the distraction of watching his claim or he'd probably be staring at Mercy. Hugo probably wouldn't take kindly to that.

In short order, they ate, and Mercy made two pallets on the benches inside the mine. One on each wall.

"I'll take first watch," she offered. She walked to him and took the rifle from his hands. "My bed is the one on the right. Take it and sleep."

He was about to reject her offer when Hugo stood up and stretched. "Get to bed, boy. Mercy is good at guard duty. She won't fall asleep on the job."

"Make sure you wake me—"

"Don't you worry. You'll get your turn," Mercy interrupted. "Scoot so I can sit there and keep an eye on your things."

"What about Ole Blue?"

"She's been in camps longer than anyone. She knows to care for herself. Now, good night." Mercy stared at him until he got up. Then she promptly sat down and ignored both men.

GREG

Dawn approached, and Mercy woke as she did every morning, before the sun. It was still cold this early in the spring season. She wrapped a blanket around her shoulders and started a fire. Next, she put a big pot of coffee on to boil and almost laughed at how deeply the lookout was sleeping.

Greg sure was a handsome man. His hair was nut brown. The color of an acorn, she mused. He sported a well-trimmed beard. He didn't have the hardened look of a miner yet. There were still smiles left inside of him. His broad shoulders would be a help to him. He didn't smell as bad as the rest, yet, either.

He'd be safe once the sun was up. No one would shoot in the morning hours. There were too many people around. Did he know the dangers that faced him out here? He didn't look too green. There were callouses on his hands, so he wasn't a milk toast miner. His teeth weren't black or missing, so he wasn't a man who paid no mind toward caring for himself.

His eyes opened, and he caught her staring. Her face heated as she quickly turned away.

"I guess I fell asleep." He scrambled to his feet and quickly pulled the flap back then sighed in relief. "My things are all still there."

Her lips twitched into a smile. "You got lucky. Remind me to never ask you to guard me." She couldn't help but tease him.

Greg smiled back, warming her. "Well, I wouldn't blame you. I don't have a proven record here yet."

His eyes matched his smile which was unusual among the miners, except for the ones who struck it big.

After she poured some coffee, she handed it to him. "We'll

have our coffee and then get your tent set up. After that you start digging. Am I going too fast for you? You look lost."

"Not at all. I'm just absorbing everything you're saying. At what angle do I dig?"

He tilted his head as though he thought she wouldn't have the answer. "A hard forty-five degrees and as wide as ours is. Then you'll want to dig in a straight line. You'll need lumber in a few days or so."

"You're quite knowledgeable for a… I'm sorry. I'm going to have to get used to the fact you know more than me and you're female."

"Female she is, and keep your mitts to yourself or I'll have to shoot you," Hugo said from his bunk.

"How many have you had to shoot already?" Greg asked.

"None."

Mercy shook her head. "Only because I chase them away before he gets a chance. A man who wants to court me will arrive with flowers someday."

"Go on, the two of ya. Get the tent up, and Greg, you let Mercy show you where to dig. She's usually pretty lucky at picking a spot."

Mercy put on a gun belt, checked her pistol for bullets and then grabbed her hat and coat before stepping out into the cold morning air. Her breath made little white puffs as she pulled on her coat. Work would warm her up.

She walked over to Greg's claim. Well, Greg had missed a person pulling his stake out of the ground. Men! She picked up the pickaxe and turned in a circle for all to see and then she sank it back into the ground. She tipped her hat to the small audience that had gathered.

"Listen up. There was shooting last night over this here claim. It's been claimed, so no more shooting if you know what's good for you." She pulled her coat back enough to expose her gun. "I don't know where a lot of you are from, but here we stick to the code of no stealing from a miner and no claim jumping." A few men narrowed their eyes at her and a few smiled. The others just shook their heads. She stood there until Greg joined her. By then most of the men were gone.

"They respect you." There was a sense of awe on Greg's face.

"Of course they do. Like I told you, I'm a hard worker, and that's what is respected most out here." She patted her holster. "That and my gun. Now don't listen to any rumors of me shooting a man in the head. I mean, I shot at his head, but I only got his ear."

Greg laughed. "What?"

"He came into the mine and tried to have his way with me and ended up running away with only half an ear. Oh my stars, talk about a lot of blood!"

She frowned. "Why do you stare at me like that, Greg? You would have shot anyone who came into your claim and put his hands on you!"

Greg stopped looking so amused. "You're right I would have. Glad he didn't hurt you. Is he still in camp?"

"My pa would have killed him if he hadn't skedaddled."

Mercy pulled a tent out from his pile of belongings. "Let's get started. I have a mine of my own to tend to."

She'd shocked him. She could tell by the look on his face. She wanted to laugh, but she put on her poker face. She didn't need another miner to think they were meant to be together. It got irksome, and one of these days her pa was going to have to up and kill one of them. She tried everything she could to discourage the men. With Greg, she was having fun at his expense. He actually seemed to be a good man, though time would tell.

"I do know how to put the tent up, you know," Greg grabbed the polls and followed her.

GREG

Mercy stepped back and looked at their handy work. "It'll stay up. Stop over if you need anything else."

"Wait, where am I supposed to dig?"

"Inside the tent for now."

His brow furrowed.

"Look, start on the left side and put the dirt on the back right side. You don't want anyone to see what might be on the piece of land. If you find gold keep your mouth closed about it. What you are actually doing is carving out the mouth and living quarters of your mine. Dig down and out toward the opening to your tent. You'll want to be able to walk into your mine. Make it as big as mine and then shore it up with lumber. Then you dig your shaft into the earth. I'll stop by later to see how you're doing."

"Thank you, Mercy. You've been a great help."

Her face grew warm. "Well, it will be nice to have a normal person next to us for a change. There's food at Ima's tent. It's over yonder. Most eat there, and in turns. You watch someone's claim and then they watch yours. Got it?"

"I got it."

"See you later, then."

Greg admired her as she walked away. She was so different from the women back home. Heck, she couldn't be any older than fifteen or sixteen, yet she had an air of confidence about her. But if she was so lucky picking the digging place, then why were they still trying to find gold after all these years? Or maybe they'd found it and Hugo gambled it away?

Greg had seen a lot of that in Hang Town. In fact, he'd seen an awful lot more in that mining town. But at least there were buildings there. Here, the town consisted of a big muddy street with mostly tents serving as businesses, the

GREG

largest being the saloon. He'd peeked in and got more than an eyeful and left. He'd never seen women in such state of undress. Weren't they cold?

He'd seen men in expensive suits buying mining gear mixing in with the miners dressed in rags. Gold fever hit all kinds. He saw riches to be made besides gold. Lumber mills, supplies, homemade food were gold mines of their own. First he'd try his hand at mining.

Picking up his spade, he dug and dug. He was glad of Mercy's advice. He had thought he'd just dig here and there or pan for gold even. But the streams were played out, and a lot of the surface dirt had been gone through. The only thing left was going into the earth.

"Hey, Greg, It's Hugo," called out his neighbor. "Don't shoot."

Greg leaned heavily on the shovel and waited for Hugo to come in.

Hugo whistled. "By golly. You work fast. You'll want to grade the front a bit. If it rains you don't want the water sloshing into your mine. Come take a look at ours after the noon meal. That's why I'm here, to take you with me."

Greg looked down at his dirty clothes. "I'll need to change."

Hugo laughed. "You look cleaner than most. Come on you'll see. Ima makes the best pie this side of the Rocky Mountains. Now, you can pay by the day, but she'd rather be paid by the week. Sometimes miners forget to eat and she doesn't think she should be out of money for food she cooked and they missed. She's a nice gal. Keep your hands off her."

Greg nodded as they trekked down the hill to a big tent. He spotted Ima and she was no gal. She looked to be old as dirt. Maybe to Hugo she was still young. She rushed over to meet Greg. She wore trousers and she was as skinny as a starved rabbit.

"Howdy do?" She stuck out her hand and Greg shook it.

"No spitting, go light on the cussin' and wait your turn. Those are the rules. I'll make up more as needed. How'll you be paying?"

"By the week, ma'am."

Ima smiled brightly. "Good idea. Seeing as it's Thursday and I collect money on Saturday I'll only charge you for half a week."

Greg started to protest, but Hugo stuck his elbow against Greg's ribs.

"Sounds fair to me." He dug into his pocket, took out some cash and handed it to her. He expected some change but he wasn't offered any.

"Go ahead and go through the chow line. You only get to go through once so pile up your plates—except for dessert. That you can have only one of. Coffee is on each table. If you bring your own tin cup and plate, I give a discount. Enjoy your meal."

She hurried around to the other side of the table that held the food and doled out the mashed potatoes while making small talk with each man. Greg watched as most piled meat five or six pieces high, leaving room for not much more. Hugo roared in laughter and Greg turned to see what was going on. Ima was hitting a man with her spoon.

"You scoundrel! That plate is bigger than any of the others. No cheating. You get this one warning, then it's cold cans of beans for you! Put some of that meat back then go eat." She muttered under her breath as she shook her head. She shook her head so hard her braids of gray hair shook back and forth too.

GREG

The tables were made of long planks of wood, the seats roughhewn benches that resembled sawhorses. Greg nodded at the group of men who sat at the table Hugo led him to. They all quickly looked away. *Friendly crowd.*

"Boys, this here is Greg. He has his claim next to mine. Funny thing, someone was shooting at him last night. Did any of you see anything?" Hugo put his tray down and sat.

Greg did the same as he glanced from one man to another. No one looked the least bit guilty. They were all different shapes and sizes, but all he saw was the caked mud on their faces. It was going to take a bit to figure out who was who.

Hugo took a big bit of ham and began to introduce the others to Greg. "That one there is Smitz, then Mac, Glad, and Longster."

"Nice to meet you."

They grunted and continued to eat.

"Don't you want to know why they call me Glad?" asked a tall, stocky man.

"Because you're pleasant?"

Everyone at the table laughed except for Glad.

"It's short for Gladiator." Glad seemed to be waiting for some response, but Greg wasn't sure what.

"That's very interesting."

"Just don't get in my way," Glad warned in a gruff tone.

Greg nodded. Was he given that name or had he made it up to sound tough?

"I heard the shots, rifle shots last night," Smitz said, his voice low and soft. "They came from up high on the opposite hill."

"Someone opened their flap about gold being here and now we have all the riffraff coming in."

Greg thought of his ma. She'd consider the men at the table riffraff.

GREG

"I'm taking him under my wing," Hugo announced.

Each man gave Hugo a solemn nod like it was some code of the miners. Whatever it was, Greg was grateful.

"Did you meet Mercy yet?" The man named Mac asked. Mac had two front gold teeth and from what Greg could tell they were the only teeth he had.

Greg chewed his food before answering. "Yes I did. She's a lovely person, and she helped me tremendously."

"Saved your bacon, did she?" Longster asked.

"She sure did."

They finished eating and headed back.

"You looked for gold while you were digging didn't you?" Hugo asked.

"Of course I did."

Hugo nodded. "Good. Next thing is to put the dirt outside of the tent so you have somewhere to lay your head.

Greg looked at him.

"The sides of the tents roll up. Just shove the dirt to the outside. This will serve two purposes. One you have room in the tent. Two, people see that you didn't find anything and will hopefully leave you be for a while. Keep your gun handy at night and keep you lamp low. You don't want to make yourself a target. In another day or so you can move your tent to the side and start shoring up your entrance. Come on to my mine. I'll show you what I mean about grading."

They walked through the flaps to Hugo's mine and both men quickly turned their backs toward Mercy. She'd been changing her shirt and she didn't wear undergarments. Greg didn't see much, but he got the impression of creamy soft skin, and he caught the slightest glimpse of her curves.

"Pa, you're supposed to whistle. You can turn around now. I'm clothed."

Greg figured she'd be the one blushing but it was he who felt heat on his cheeks. "Sorry about that, Mercy."

"No harm done." She gave him one of her warm smiles. "How's the digging going? Are you rich yet?"

"Fine and no. I'm here to see about grading to avoid flooding."

Mercy began to explain how it was done while Hugo went into the mine with his pickaxe. Greg listened to her in fascination. She sounded more like an engineer than a miner.

"You're educated."

"You noticed?"

"You know boys don't like smart girls, at least that's what my sister Scarlett says."

"I don't care, never did. I'm too smart for that kind of logic."

Greg laughed. "I do think we can be good friends, Mercy."

"As long as you don't try to get too friendly we'll do quite well together. Now scoot. I have a mine to work."

"Yes, ma'am." Greg wanted to smile as he walked back to his tent, but he put on his best expressionless face. Happiness usually equaled a gold strike around here, and he didn't want to put himself or Mercy in danger.

All he thought of while he shoveled the dirt out of his tent was Mercy. She was so unlike anyone he'd ever met, her presence in mining country so unexpected. But mining for gold was just the adventure he'd been looking for.

"Well, hello good looking."

Greg startled, grabbed his gun, and spun around. Standing inside his tent was a beautiful blond woman with not nearly enough clothes on. He swallowed hard, not knowing exactly where to look.

"Hello, ma'am."

She laughed. "Your ma must have taught you some nice manners. My name is Shelly. I just wanted to say hello. I like to greet all the new men."

GREG

"Nice to meet you. I'm Greg Settler. Are you in camp with your husband?"

"Aren't you a young one. Unjaded, I like that. No I work in the saloon tent. I was hoping I'd see you there later. The first one is free."

His jaw dropped and his face heated. "Excuse me?"

She fluttered her eyelashes at him and gave him a coy smile. "The first drink, silly."

"Would you like to put my coat on? It doesn't seem—"

"I put on an extra petticoat for the walk over. I'm fine. I usually don't make house calls but in your case I could make an exception." She walked closer with each word until she had her hand on his cheek. "I'd like us to be friends."

He took a step back. "A person can never have too many friends. Listen Shelly, I need to get back to work, but it was nice to meet you."

She frowned and looked around his mine. "Maybe you wouldn't be able to afford me. Have you found any gold yet?"

"Not yet but one can hope."

Continue Reading

ABOUT THE AUTHOR

Sexy Cowboys and the Women Who Love Them...
Finalist in the 2012 and 2015 RONE Awards.
Top Pick, Five Star Series from the Romance Review.
Kathleen Ball writes contemporary and historical western romance with great emotion and
memorable characters. Her books are award winners and have appeared on best sellers lists including: Amazon's Best Seller's List, All Romance Ebooks, Bookstrand, Desert Breeze Publishing and Secret Cravings Publishing Best Sellers list. She is the recipient of eight Editor's Choice Awards, and The Readers' Choice Award for Ryelee's Cowboy.
Winner of the Lear diamond award Best Historical Novel- Cinders' Bride
There's something about a cowboy

facebook.com/kathleenballwesternromance

twitter.com/kballauthor

instagram.com/author_kathleenball

OTHER BOOKS BY KATHLEEN

Lasso Spring Series
Callie's Heart
Lone Star Joy
Stetson's Storm

Dawson Ranch Series
Texas Haven
Ryelee's Cowboy

Cowboy Season Series
Summer's Desire
Autumn's Hope
Winter's Embrace
Spring's Delight

Mail Order Brides of Texas
Cinder's Bride
Keegan's Bride
Shane's Bride
Tramp's Bride
Poor Boy's Christmas

Oregon Trail Dreamin'
We've Only Just Begun
A Lifetime to Share
A Love Worth Searching For

So Many Roads to Choose

The Settlers
Greg

Juan

Scarlett

Mail Order Brides of Spring Water
Tattered Hearts

Shattered Trust

Glory's Groom

Battered Soul

Romance on the Oregon Trail
Cora's Courage

Luella's Longing

Dawn's Destiny

Terra's Trial

Candle Glow and Mistletoe

The Kabvanagh Brothers
Teagan: Cowboy Strong

Quinn: Cowboy Risk

Brogan: Cowboy Pride

Sullivan: Cowboy Protector

Donnell: Cowboy Scrutiny

Murphy: Cowboy Deceived

Fitzpatrick: Cowboy Reluctant

Angus: Cowboy Bewildered

The Greatest Gift

Love So Deep
Luke's Fate
Whispered Love
Love Before Midnight
I'm Forever Yours
Finn's Fortune
Glory's Groom

Made in the USA
Las Vegas, NV
21 October 2020

10217792R00095